Death at the Duck Pond

A Finch & Fischer Mystery

J. New

This is a work of fiction. Names, characters, businesses, places, events and incidents are either products of the author's imagination or used in a fictitious manner. Any resemblance to actual persons, living or dead, or actual events is purely coincidental.

Cover illustration: WILLIAM WEBB

Cover typography: MARIAH SINCLAIR

BOOKS BY J. NEW

The Finch & Fischer Mysteries

Decked in the Hall

Death at the Duck Pond

Battered to Death

The Yellow Cottage Vintage Mysteries

The Yellow Cottage Mystery (FREE)

An Accidental Murder

The Curse of Arundel Hall

A Clerical Error

The Riviera Affair

Full details on these and future books in the series can be found on the website:

www.jnewwrites.com

Table of Contents

One 5
Two 17
Three 27
Four 37
Five 48
Six 57
Seven 66
Eight 78
Nine 86
Ten 95
Eleven 104
Twelve 118
Thirteen 136
Fourteen 148
Fifteen 166
Sixteen 184

One

Strangers to the village of Cherrytree Downs had been known to gawk, overcome with curiosity, at the crowd of locals gathered around the converted VW camper-van parked by the village green on a Thursday, week in, week out. Anyone taking a closer look soon realised its location in the prime parking space beside the picnic area was no accident, the nearby tables and benches doubling as a waiting and browsing area for the steady stream of people entering and leaving the van from morning until mid-afternoon, when it trundled on its way. The buzz of conversation, laughter and sometimes raised voices that filled the centre of the village when the van was in situ, rain or shine, were all testament to its importance in the community. To what, one may have wondered, did the van owe its lure?

In the midst of it all could be found Penny Finch, mobile librarian and owner of the van, doling out book recommendations and down-to-earth conversation in equal measure. Her constant companion, Fischer, a rescue pup, was also on hand, providing entertainment and making himself available for cuddles. Ever since Penny had adopted Fischer several months before, she was sure the library van attendance had increased.

"That'll be twenty pence, please, Mrs Nelson. I'm afraid your books are late again," Penny said, smiling at the elderly woman facing her. Popular as well as fair, Penny wasn't afraid to pull any punches, especially when it came to library fines. Certain people were regular offenders, and if she didn't follow through and insist on payment, chaos would reign. Her fiancé, Edward, scoffed at what he considered the futility of the fines system, but Penny disagreed.

Mrs Nelson scowled back at her. Penny didn't know her very well, she was a newcomer to the village, but what she'd seen of her so far hadn't been favourable. Cantankerous was the word which sprang to mind. "Twenty pence? It's not my fault I couldn't bring them back on time. The weather's been awful. I've barely been out the door."

Penny's smile remained fixed in place. "I understand, Mrs Nelson. But I have to enforce the rules for everyone, or else I'll get into trouble."

The old woman pulled out her purse, grumbling all the while. "I still think it's ridiculous, penalising seniors. I can barely survive on my pension as it is." She shoved a handful of coppers at Penny, her face sour. "Here. I've a good mind to complain. I had none of this nonsense in Africa. *There*, I was trusted with the books I wished to read."

Penny counted out the coins as she placed them through

the slot in the lid of the fines tin. As she had suspected, they fell short of the full amount. "Do you have another two pence, Mrs Nelson?" Having seen the wad of notes stuffed inside Mrs Nelson's purse, the diamond earrings and the antique brooch affixed to the lapel of her cashmere coat, Penny couldn't understand her vociferous objection to the fines system, she was obviously a woman of means. But she wasn't intimidated by the defiant glare she received in return.

Another coin was duly produced, and Mrs Nelson left in a huff, but not before Penny had thanked her politely. She looked up at the next customer and beamed in recognition.

"Hello, Mr Kelly. How are you, this grey afternoon? Did you have a nice time in Florida?"

Penny had recently become good friends with Mr Kelly, the retired head teacher of the local primary school, when the two of them had helped the police solve the murder of a local woman in the run up to Christmas. In the weeks since, she had not seen Mr Kelly on the library van's visits to his home village of Rowan Downs on Mondays and had heard he was away.

Mr Kelly patted Fischer, who upon recognising the voice of a friend had appeared at his ankles, produced a treat from his pocket and was rewarded with one of the little dogs tricks, a 'high-five' and a bark of hello.

"It was marvellous, Penny. Did me the world of good. My arthritis plays up no end in this weather," he motioned to the drizzle outside. "I'm not sure I'd like to spend the whole winter there like my sister and her friends, but a couple of weeks in the sun in January makes a very pleasant change from cold, wet Blighty, let me tell you."

"I'm so glad you enjoyed it. I've got a few new mystery books in stock, if you'd like to have a look?"

Mr Kelly's eyes twinkled. "I would, very much, but I'll wait until you're in Rowan Downs on Monday, if that's all right? It'll save me carrying them, as I'm off for a walk before meeting my daughter later. I'm not one for New Year's resolutions, but I'm aiming for five thousand steps a day ever since the doctor insisted I exercise my new hip as much as possible. I even have one of these." He pushed up his coat sleeve to reveal a pedometer strapped to his left wrist, no bigger than a watch. "It's a marvellous bit of kit. Anyway, I wondered if Fischer would like to join me?"

Fischer yelped and wagged his tail before taking a spin around Mr Kelly's legs.

"There's your answer, Mr Kelly, he understood every word you said." Penny chuckled. "He's making me dizzy just looking at him. I'll get you his lead." Reaching into the front of the van, she glanced at the time on the clock on the dashboard as she did so. "I've to go to Winstoke soon to restock the van," she said, turning back to fix Fischer's lead to his harness. "Do you mind dropping him off at my parents' house when you're finished? I'll pick him up when I get back to Cherrytree Downs later."

With the exception of her time at university, Penny had

lived in the village all her life. City living did not appeal to her, and despite having travelled widely on holiday there was no other place she would rather be. Certain of her own mind, she had never felt she was missing out or had a desire to live elsewhere. Her small thatched cottage had a view of the green and her parents lived several streets away in the larger home she had grown up in. With her favourite people, her best friend Susie included, all living within a small radius, she considered herself fortunate.

"I'll do that, no problem." Mr Kelly tugged Fischer's lead. "Have a nice weekend, Penny. I'll see you on Monday."

"You too, and thanks." Penny turned to Fischer, "Be a good boy, you hear me? No pulling on your lead." The small Jack Russell Terrier ignored her, skipping down the van steps ahead of his walking companion. As Mr Kelly made his way out, holding the handrail, Fischer jumped impatiently up and down, to the delight of the people outside watching.

"Fischer's such a darling," Katy Lowry, the barmaid at the Pig and Fiddle said, as she handed Penny two books to be checked out. A keen romance reader, she favoured chunky tomes with high levels of heat, affectionately known as bonkbusters, and devoured them as soon as they appeared on the shelves. With the books now in her possession for the week, she gave a hearty wave, jumped down the steps and ran across the green to begin her shift at the pub.

Penny's final customer was the elderly Mrs Davenport, a lover of historical fiction. As she handed Penny her choice for that week she leaned closer.

"Penny, I couldn't help but overhear your conversation with Katy. Could you tell me, what actually is a bonkbuster?"

Penny smiled and beckoned her closer, whispering the answer in her ear.

"My, my, how astonishing. I've never heard the term before."

"A word for the new millennium, Mrs Davenport."

"Is it in the dictionary, dear?"

"I believe so, yes."

"Well, I shall purchase a new one immediately. It will certainly make my weekly scrabble games much more interesting!"

Penny's drive home from the main library in Winstoke that evening was slow, despite the short distance. The camper van was stuck behind a tractor for most of the five-mile trip, which provided her with the chance to listen to the Beginner's Italian CD her parents had bought her for Christmas. She repeated the words after the instructor attempting to mimic his accent. There were no overtaking spots along the winding road but she didn't mind in the least. Life in the slow lane was no hardship when one lived in the moment and was happy to give way to a rabbit or a fox on the roadside. The commuters whizzing in and out of the six villages that made up Hampsworthy Downs in their flashy cars never ceased to amaze her. What was the point of living somewhere so beautiful, if one was in too much of a hurry to appreciate it? Their irresponsibility also made her blood boil. It was dangerous, not only for other car users and pedestrians, but for the wildlife.

Penny parked the van outside her cottage in its usual spot beside the blue Ford Fiesta belonging to her neighbour. The row of five quaint cottages did not have driveways or garages, and there was no designated on-street parking, but residents were respectful about leaving a space outside someone else's home if that person had a car. The fact that the library van took up a larger space than the neighbours' vehicles was never a problem, as a couple of the older residents didn't drive and only needed a parking space when they had visitors.

"Hello, Mrs Montague," she said to an elderly woman who was walking past as she opened the garden gate. "You're early this evening, or am I terribly late?"

Penny and Fischer often bumped into Mrs Montague on their evening walk after dinner, which took them across the village green, around the duck pond, and as far as the church and back. Mrs Montague was known to drive into the village in her Land Rover and do a circuit of the village at a similar time, before heading back to her manor house on the hill overlooking Cherrytree Downs.

Mrs Montague stopped and smiled. "Good evening, Penelope. Probably a bit of both. I'm meeting someone later, so I thought I'd take a quick scoot to the Pig and Fiddle first and treat myself to a bite of dinner."

"That sounds lovely." The food at the village pub, was legendary, and had won several gastropub awards. Penny and Edward often went there for lunch on a Sunday, but rarely during the week. "Thursday night's the pub quiz, so it will be busy."

Mrs Montague flashed her a girlish grin. "I know. All the better. I'm pretty good at general knowledge, if I say so myself. Not that I'm staying for long, of course." She raised an arm to tuck her scarf into her collar, revealing several large rings on her bony hand. "I'd best be off. Good night, Penelope, dear. Good night, Fischer."

"Good night, Mrs Montague. Enjoy yourself."

Penny found herself smiling as she let herself into the house. Mrs Montague's joie de vivre was contagious. She picked up the post from the mat and after flicking through the envelopes to see if there was anything of interest, set them on the hall table. It looked like bills and marketing offers, which meant the envelopes would remain unopened for days. All of Penny's bills were paid by direct debit, meaning she never had to worry about missing a payment. Edward checked her finances every quarter as well, to ensure there was nothing amiss. It was one of the perks of being engaged to an accountant.

In the living room, she pulled on a heat-resistant mitt

and opened the wood burning stove to stoke the embers before adding a couple of logs to get it going again. Then, only after she had wandered into the kitchen and flipped the switch on the kettle, did she go back into the hallway and take off her coat, hanging it up on its peg. Several minutes later she was ensconced in an armchair in front of the fire, a cup of cinnamon and rooibos tea in hand, and a book on her knee. She had arranged to pick Fischer up from her parents' house after she had eaten, but first, she wanted to savour her favourite part of the week. Much as she loved her job, she adored getting home from work on Thursdays, because it was the start of her weekend. Reducing her working week had been an unexpected consequence of being employed by the cash-strapped Hantchester Borough Council, but it had turned out well and Penny wasn't complaining.

Penny stretched out her arm to silence the alarm clock on the bedside table and pulled the covers tight, enjoying another couple of minutes of sleepy comfort before the snooze feature set the alarm ringing again. Pulling herself up and swinging her legs out, her feet found their way into the cosy slippers waiting by the side of the bed. She switched off the alarm, turned on the lamp, and padded into the bathroom. The sound of the toilet flushing was Fischer's wakeup call, and she knew he would be waiting for her, ear cocked, in his basket in the living room by the fire when she descended the stairs.

"How's my little Fish Face this morning?" she said, crouching down to stroke his warm fur. "Pretending to be asleep, are we?" Fischer opened his eyes and rolled on his back for a tummy rub, his tail thumping in anticipation. "Come on, little man, let's have breakfast and then we'll get ready for our walk."

Even before she had rescued Fischer from certain death several months earlier, Penny had always been an early riser, so sticking to their routine wasn't hard on the days she did not work. Susie had been shocked when she learned Penny got up at 6.45am every day without fail and tried to talk her out of it.

"Penny, are you serious?" Susie's eyes were the size of saucers. "The least you could do is allow yourself an extra half an hour's beauty sleep on your days off. At our age, goodness knows we need it. Ever since both my children stopped waking me up at the crack of dawn, I've grabbed every last second of slumber I can get. Especially recently."

"Well I have Fischer to think of," Penny reasoned. "And your weekdays are a lot more manic than mine, so it's no wonder you're exhausted by the weekend." Susie was separated from her husband and as well as her single-parenting duties, had a job at the local newspaper as a Junior Reporter. Penny knew her friend loved the work but struggled sometimes like any working mother. She admired how Susie was coping, despite the emotional and financial stress she had been going through since her husband had left her.

"Well, if you ever need a break, send Fischer around to my house. Billy and Ellen adore him. They'd love a dog, but they know it's not a good time right now. Fischer can be their surrogate pet."

Penny had agreed, if only to keep Susie happy. She could not imagine ever needing a break from her furry sidekick.

After seeing to Fischer, she was adding a spoonful of Manuka honey to her bowl of porridge when her phone buzzed, and Susie's name flashed up on the screen. Given the early hour, Penny sensed something was wrong before she answered the call. Susie would be up for work and busy getting her children out to school, but there was no way she would be telephoning her at this time of the morning unless it was urgent. She held the device to her ear, her heart pounding.

"Susie? Is something wrong?"

Susie sounded breathless. "Yes. Have you looked out of your front window this morning?"

Penny started walking towards the living room. "No, I haven't even opened the curtains yet. It's still dark. Why?"

"I'm on my way over there now to start covering a story for The Gazette. Billy's going to walk Ellen to school. Quick, tell me, what can you see?"

Penny pulled back a heavy velvet curtain and peered outside. "Oh, my word." A small crowd was gathered at the edge of the village green, which was illuminated by several wrought-iron lamp posts and the flashing lights of a police car and an ambulance. “The green’s closed off with police tape. PC Bolton is there, and an ambulance, and several more people.” She squinted through the glass to make them out. “I think it’s Dr Jones from The Rough Spot and the postman, and some paramedics. Oh, and a man in shorts. What’s going on? It’s a wonder I didn’t hear the sirens.”

“There was a 999 call just after five this morning, so they’ve been there for a while.” Susie’s voice cracked. “Oh, Penny. It’s bad news, I’m afraid.”

“Go on.” Penny held her breath.

“An elderly woman has been found dead in the duck pond. The body hasn’t been formally identified, but apparently, it’s Myrtle Montague.”

Two

When Fischer turned to go right as they exited the garden gate a short while later, Penny hesitated, and tugged his lead. The usual route for their morning walk was across the green, halfway around the duck pond, and cutting out through the lane that led to the row of shops that served the village.

The newsagent's and the Bakewell bakery both opened at seven in the morning, the Evans' baking their own bread rather than buying it in. And Penny could set her watch by Mr Jackson, the greengrocer, unloading his van when he returned from the fresh produce market in Winstoke every morning at seven-fifteen. The hairdressing salon, quirkily named The Lock Smith, and the butcher's opened later, at nine o'clock. From the shops, Penny and Fischer would normally loop back to Penny's house via Cherrytree Row, lined with the mature trees that gave the village its name. Every May when their blossom reached full bloom the village was illuminated by a riot of pink for several weeks.

That morning however, there was no question of getting

access to the green or the duck pond. The number of onlookers had grown to a small crowd, and what little traffic there was at that time of the morning had slowed to a halt as drivers rolled down their windows to find out the cause of the delay. Penny spotted Susie, notebook and pen in hand, talking to the man in shorts she had seen through the window earlier.

"We'll have to go the long way today, Fischer, not that you'll mind in the slightest. There's been a terrible accident." She thought of Mrs Montague, standing in the very same spot outside her gate the evening before, and how excited she had been about heading out. A sociable woman, she had been widowed a couple of years earlier, and involved herself in village life to the full.

"I like to keep busy," she had confided to Penny one afternoon, when she had called in to the van for permission to leave flyers advertising a charity coffee morning she was hosting at the manor. "When you get to my age, every day is too precious a gift to waste. I miss dear old Daniel, of course, but he wouldn't want me moping around. And I'm finding the book I've been reading about the Big Bang and black holes absolutely fascinating. Learning keeps the grey matter active, don't you think?"

"I think reading's beneficial at any age," Penny had replied. "It has so many benefits. For instance, if only more people would sit down with a good book to ease their stress instead of popping pills, the world would be happier place.

Not to mention the resulting savings for the National Health Service. Unfortunately, many doctors are so stressed themselves, it's quicker and makes their lives easier to keep writing prescriptions instead of discussing the alternatives with their patients."

Penny remembered how Mrs Montague had patted her arm, saying, "I can see you feel passionately about it, Penelope, and you must try not to be discouraged. You do a wonderful job in this little van of yours, and on a shoestring budget, it's very much appreciated by everyone who uses the service. Long may it last."

Penny was brought back to the present by Fischer bouncing around at her feet, eager to be off. "Let's go, Fish Face," she whispered, her eyes smarting. "First stop, the bakery, I think. You don't understand, little man, but I'm in need of some comfort food. There was a nice old lady who was very fond of you, and I don't think we'll be seeing her again."

At the Bakewell, any faint hope Penny was clinging to, that Susie was mistaken about the identity of the body was put to rest by Mrs Evans.

"Hello, Penny. Did you hear about Mrs Montague?" Mrs Evans' hair was tucked inside a net she wore in the bakery, giving her head a misshapen look. Outside work, her bottle blonde bouffant was her trademark feature.

Penny nodded. "Susie phoned me earlier. She's over at the green now, interviewing people for the newspaper." Her voice faltered. "Are they positive it was Mrs Montague, and not someone else?"

Mrs Evans' look of sadness matched Penny's. "I'm afraid so. It was Sam Dawson who found the body in the pond, when he was out jogging first thing. Actually, it was his dog, Rufus, who kicked up a commotion. The light from the lampposts just about reaches the duck pond in the dark. Rufus jumped into the water and Sam waded in after him and dragged poor Myrtle's body out. He knows her from the church. He said she weighed like lead, even though she was such a petite woman."

Penny shuddered. "I'll have a pain au chocolate, please, and a strong cup of tea, to sit in." The bakery had a counter along the window with high stools, and pets were allowed.

"You go on, love, I'll bring it over. You've gone very pale."

"Thank you." Penny gave her a grateful smile.

The stream of customers coming in and out of the bakery and fussing over Fischer gave Penny the opportunity to nurse her tea and eat her pastry in silence, apart from exchanging quick greetings with those she knew. The talk on everyone's lips was of Myrtle, and what a tragic accident to have befallen such a nice old lady, the general consensus being that she had tripped into the pond in the dark and drowned. Snippets of conversation drifted in and out of Penny's hearing, but she did not engage in any of the gossip.

"Saw her in the Pig and Fiddle last night, what a shame," said one. "She gave our team one of the answers in the quiz."

"She probably had too much to drink," said another. "Maybe she'd been at the cooking sherry before she came out."

"Celia raised the alarm when she went to wake her, and found her bed hadn't been slept in." This, from a voice Penny recognised, Dr Jones, the vet, who she had seen on the green earlier. She knew he was referring to Celia Higgins, Mrs Montague's live-in housekeeper, who had worked at the manor for as long as Penny could remember. "Sam had already found the body by then. Poor Celia's in a terrible state."

A niggling thought crossed Penny's mind that she felt guilty for even dwelling upon, but the more she tried to push it out of her head, the more prominent it became. Was it terrible of her for trying to remember if Myrtle had any library books out on loan, and wondering, if so, whether they would ever be returned? Most books were never seen again after people died, and in the circumstances, it was Penny's policy not to go looking for them. However, the lack of library funding was a serious issue, one which sometimes kept her awake at night. Considering the ageing local population, it was a theoretical possibility that at some point there would be no books left.

Having debated the dilemma in the past with Edward, his input had been unhelpful. "An undertaking to retrieve the missing books is unlikely to be effective, since the culprits are dead." After a pause, he continued, "Not to mention, the incurring expense to follow them up would not be cost effective. I've always said the fines for late books are much too low, there's no incentive to returning them." He loved to labour the fines point at any opportunity.

Penny vacated her seat in the Bakewell when a queue formed, parents squeezing inside after dropping off their children at the primary school. The Friday morning buzz was familiar, but the topic of conversation too distressing for her to enjoy her pastry, which she did not finish.

Outside, Fischer seemed to pick up on her mood, and he held back, walking alongside her rather than bolting ahead in his usual fashion. The school playground was empty and silent, the morning bell having already rung, and they walked the length of the black railings before turning into the street where her parents lived.

Penny mustered a smile as Fischer's pace quickened. "You recognise where we are, don't you? Calm down, we'll be there in a minute." Even so, by the time she rang her parents' doorbell she was out of breath, having had to jog most of the way in order to keep up with her exuberant little dog.

Her mother answered the door, looking flustered. "I'm so glad you're here. What terrible news." She ushered Penny inside, but not before Fischer had squeezed in first. Penny dropped his lead and watched him bound down the hallway. "Your father's in the kitchen, still not dressed. He can't believe it."

"Neither can I." Penny followed her mother into the kitchen, taking off her coat as she went. She hung it on the back of a chair and sat down at the kitchen table beside her father. "Hi, Dad."

Albert Finch looked across at Penny whilst stroking Fischer, who was settled in his lap. "What's the latest? Your mother saw the commotion when she was getting the paper earlier. Is it true about Mrs Montague?"

Penny recounted what she had heard from Mrs Evans and the other customers at the Bakewell. "I spoke to her last night," she said. "She was in great spirits. I never would have imagined it would be the last time I would see her alive."

Sheila Finch had been listening from where she was standing at the sink. She frowned. "And I saw her on Monday at Winstoke Leisure Centre, at the ladies' swimming session in the morning. Which is why I think it strange that she should have drowned. She was a highly competent swimmer."

Albert adjusted his glasses. "That's a good point. And the duck pond's neither big nor deep. Maybe she hit her head or something. I don't think she was much of a drinker, whatever anyone says. I know she was getting on in years, but she wasn't that much older than me. I could probably work it out, but it's too early in the morning." He made a face at Fischer, who was hanging on to his every word.

"She was still full of life, whatever her age," Sheila said. "I suppose that means her son will be making an appearance shortly. He never visited his mother much, shame on him.

What's his name again?"

"Milo," Penny said. "I'd completely forgotten about him. You're right, I haven't seen him in years." Older than Penny, she recalled Myrtle's son had attended boarding school outside the area. Any time she had seen him when they were younger, he had been accompanied by loud upper crust types who had a tendency to mock the more down to earth locals.

"He was at his father's funeral, if I recall," Albert said. "But he didn't stick around and left straight afterwards. I don't know the details, but I suspect there was a bit of a family fallout at some point over the years. Whatever Milo did to upset his parents, it wasn't in his back yard, so to speak, and Myrtle and Daniel kept it under wraps. Might be nothing, but Myrtle was a fair woman. I'd say she wouldn't be rattled easily, so it must have had some substance."

Sheila pulled the plug out of the sink and the dishwater made a gurgling sound as it swirled down the drain, causing Fischer's head to perk up.

"Why don't you go and get dressed, Dad, and I'll help Mum down here? Then we can go to Thistle Grange and take a walk in the woods. Fischer would like that, and it will get us away from here until all the commotion dies down. Seeing the green cordoned off with police tape is unsettling."

Albert's face brightened. "That's a marvellous idea. Won't be long." He got up and headed towards the stairs, Fischer at his heels.

Penny jumped up and unclipped Fischer's lead, before

letting him run off again. “You sit down, Mum, and read the paper. I’ll make a fresh pot of tea and finish tidying up.”

Her mother’s house was always immaculate, but Penny needed something to do. After she had made tea and wiped the already sparkling granite worktops, she went into the living room and removed non-existent dust from the china ornaments on the mantelpiece. She ran a vacuum cleaner around the room and into the hall, putting it away again in the cupboard under the stairs. Just when she was about to tackle the downstairs bathroom, she heard her mother call her from the kitchen. “Your phone’s ringing, Penny.”

By the time Penny had located her phone in the pocket of her coat, which was no longer hanging on the chair because her mother had moved it, she had missed the call. She shoved the phone back in her pocket with a shrug. “I don’t recognise the number, it was probably a cold-call. If it’s important, they’ll call back.”

They had just set off for Thistle Grange when Penny’s phone began ringing again, and this time she answered it. Sitting in the back seat of her parents’ car, she motioned to her mother to turn down the volume on the car radio. It was a brief one-way conversation with the caller doing all the talking and Penny listening, apart from when she thanked the person at the other end of the line before ending the call.

Her mother turned around from the passenger’s seat. “Who was that, dear? Is everything all right?”

Penny gazed at her with faint surprise. “It was Mrs Montague's solicitor. He said she left an envelope for me in his care, only to be opened in the event of her death. I've to go to his office in Winstoke this afternoon to discuss it further."

For once, both of her parents were rendered speechless.

Three

"Thanks for coming with me, Susie. Am I suitably dressed for an appointment with a solicitor do you think?" Penny smoothed her skirt and buttoned up her smart black wool coat over the scarlet crew-neck jumper, which provided a spot of colour against her wavy chestnut hair. She locked the camper-van and checked her watch. They were ten minutes early, and the firm of solicitors had its own car park, but Penny liked having plenty of time to spare before important events. For her, ten minutes was cutting it fine. When she went on holiday, she always planned her arrival at the airport a little earlier than advised, just in case of an unexpected delay on the way. Ever since the time Edward had left his passport at home in his jacket and they'd had to go back for it, the two of them were in agreement on that one. Of course, Edward had blamed her for not putting his jacket in the car in the first place.

Susie eyed her with amusement. "You look very nice, although I don't see why you had to get dressed up. It's not as though you're going to court. It is intriguing, though.

Which is why my boss let me out for the afternoon, just in case your meeting adds anything to the piece I'm writing. I wonder what the mysterious letter could be about?"

"I've been asking myself the same question ever since Mr Hawkins telephoned me this morning. It's not as though I knew Mrs Montague all that well. Of course, I saw her when she came to the library van, but mostly we just talked about books." Penny turned towards the old building which had a small brass plaque engraved with the words, *Hawkins, Hawkins and Reid* to the right of the entrance. "Shall we go in?"

Susie nodded, and they walked towards the heavy oak door. "You said you and Fischer often passed her in the village on your evening walks, right? And, she was very fond of Fischer. Maybe she's left him something in her will? I'm thinking of potential headlines already; *Wealthy Widow Leaves Millions to Jack Russell Terrier.* Can you imagine the uproar if that's really the case?"

"I think you're jumping the gun a bit, don't you?" Penny said, laughing. "We never really exchanged more than pleasantries, although she did have a treat for Fischer now and then. I don't think she was quite that rich, either. Otherwise, she wouldn't have sold part of her garden to raise funds after her husband died."

"That's exactly my point, she got a fortune when Nick Staines bought the land and built that glass monstrosity next door," Susie reminded her. "It wasn't that long ago, only a couple of years. She probably still had a huge chunk of cash lying around."

Penny wrinkled her brow. "It won't be anything like that. Her son is likely to inherit everything, I should think." She pushed the door open. "Anyway, I guess we'll soon find out."

A welcome blast of warm air hit them when they stepped inside, and Penny made her way to the reception desk while Susie took a seat in the waiting area, where she rifled through the magazine rack for something to read.

"It's Penny Finch, to see Mr Hawkins," she said to the woman behind the counter, trying not to stare at her badly drawn-on eyebrows.

"Please, take a seat," the woman replied, her smile softening her face somewhat. "I'll let him know you're here."

Susie was flicking through a country homes magazine, admiring a bespoke kitchen in a converted barn, when Penny joined her on the plush two-seater sofa. "A girl can dream, right? Although, I'll take my old pine kitchen any day if it means I can hang on to the house."

"Any news on that front?" Penny knew Susie's estranged husband wanted to sell the family home, but Susie was hoping to buy him out.

"My parents have gifted me some money, and my promotion helped my mortgage prospects. It's not a done deal, but I'm hopeful."

"I'm glad things have taken a turn for the better," Penny said, proud of Susie's tenacity. As well as being a loyal friend to her over the years, Susie would have given the coat off her back to help anyone in need. She had taken a huge knock when her marriage crumbled but had maintained her dignity throughout. Penny had been more worried about her than she liked to admit, and it was a relief to hear Susie sounding so upbeat again. She smiled, "I'm not sure I'll be able to provide you with a juicy story this afternoon, but you'll be the first to know if there's anything newsworthy to report."

Before Susie could respond, they were interrupted by a bald man with a moustache whose footsteps echoed on the polished floor as he approached. "Miss Finch?" He looked at each of them in turn.

"That's me," Penny said scrambling to her feet.

"Antony Hawkins," the man said, extending his hand and greeting her with a handshake so firm, her fingers ached afterwards. "It's a pleasure to meet you, Miss Finch. Please, follow me."

Susie gave her a thumbs-up and Penny followed Mr Hawkins down the dimly-lit wood-panelled hallway into his office. He clicked the door shut and led her past a large oak desk to a small seating area with wingback leather chairs and a threadbare axminster rug on the parquet floor. The room smelled of lemon wax, coffee and old money.

When they were seated, Penny folded her hands in her lap to stop herself from fidgeting. She was not nervous, but there was apprehension in her expression as she regarded Mr Hawkins, who, sensing her concern, immediately put her at ease.

"Please, don't worry, Miss Finch." He was quietly-spoken, with a friendly face. "I realise my telephone call must have come as a bit of a surprise."

"Yes." Penny's mouth was dry, and she swallowed. "This is all a terrible shock. Everyone in the village was saddened to learn of Mrs Montague's passing. She will be missed."

Mr Hawkins nodded. "Yes, she was a unique character." He slid a cream envelope across the table towards Penny, his eyes never leaving hers. "Mrs Montague thought highly of you, Miss Finch. As it happens, she came to see me only last week. Our firm has been handling her affairs for many years, and she had a personal request to ask of you."

Penny noted he said request, not bequest, and a feeling of relief washed over her.

"Allow me to explain, if I may, although I understand it's also set out in the letter she asked me to give you."

"Please, do." Penny looked down at the envelope, and saw her name handwritten on the front in a shaky script.

"Mrs Montague's instructions were that the extensive private library in her house was to benefit the local community," Mr Hawkins continued. "Most of it is probably suitable for local educational establishments, Mr Montague having been a keen scholar throughout his lifetime. However, and this is what Myrtle came to see me about last week, she was insistent your mobile library should have first choice of any of the books you think the regular library members would like. Although I don't suppose she imagined you and I would be having this conversation quite so soon."

Penny was touched by what she was hearing, and opened her mouth to speak, but Mr Hawkins raised a finger to indicate he was not quite finished.

"That's not all. There are also instructions, subject to your agreement of course, for you to catalogue the books and allocate them to suitable beneficiaries. I understand there are some first editions which are very valuable and might be more suitable in the British Library or a museum, but you would be in charge of organising everything as required." He scrutinised her face. "Is that something you might be interested in doing, or do you need some time to think it over?"

"Goodness, I..." tears pricked Penny's eyes. She nodded, unable to speak for a moment. "I'd be honoured, Mr Hawkins. That's such a generous and thoughtful legacy. The residents of Hampsworthy Downs will be forever grateful."

Mr Hawkins beamed. "Excellent. Myrtle was an extraordinary woman. I know she'd have been delighted you've agreed to rise to the occasion, not that I think she ever doubted you would. I should add that a generous sum of money has been set aside for you to be paid for the work involved."

Penny shook her head. "That's really not necessary, Mr Hawkins. It would be a pleasure for me to do this, it's not like work at all."

"No arguments." He raised an eyebrow. "It will be rather time-consuming, labour of love or not. There's no deadline as such, but it would be preferable to clear out the books sooner rather than later."

Penny vaguely wondered if the house was being sold, not that it was any of her business. "That's no problem," she said. "I can start tomorrow, if that suits. Between evenings and weekends, I'm sure I can get it all done in a few weeks, since I don't work Fridays."

"That would be marvellous. I'll let Celia know you're coming. She'll be continuing to look after the house for now." Mr Hawkins stood up indicating the meeting was at an end, and Penny followed suit, but not before lifting the envelope from the table and placing it in her handbag.

Mr Hawkins opened the door and shook Penny's hand again before she left. "Let me know if you need anything. My secretary will be in touch with you to arrange the payment when you're done. Thank you again, Miss Finch."

"Thank you, Mr Hawkins." Penny turned and made her way back to where Susie was waiting, unable to contain her grin.

"I knew it!" Susie leapt up when she saw her and let out

a faint squeak of delight. "Was I right, is Fischer going to be a rich little doggie?"

"Ssh." Penny noticed the receptionist giving them a disapproving look and grabbed Susie by the arm. "I'll tell you outside."

In the car park, she recounted the conversation with Mr Hawkins, bouncing as she walked.

"I understand why you're excited by the prospect of getting your hands dirty with hundreds of old dusty books, and I'm pleased for you, I really am," Susie said, not as impressed as Penny by the turn of events. She sighed, "I'll just have to come up with a new headline, I suppose."

Back in the van, Susie sat in silence while Penny tore open the letter she had received from Mrs Montague, wiping a tear from her eye as she read its contents. "Look," she said when she was finished, handing the letter to Susie. "What are the chances of Mrs Montague writing this only a week ago, and then dying out of the blue? The hairs on my arms are standing on end just thinking about it." She peered in the envelope, realising there was something else in there, and pulled it out. "That's weird."

"What is?" Susie looked up from the letter and stared over at Penny. "Is that a library card?"

Penny turned the card over on her hand. "Yes. It's Mrs

Montague's library card. Why on earth would she be giving it to me?" Her heart began to race. "Something's not right, Susie."

"You mean, maybe she wasn't expecting to be reading too many more library books?"

That was exactly what had been running through Penny's mind. She bit her lip, as she connected the dots. "Think about it, Susie. Mrs Montague goes to see her lawyer with a last request a week before she dies. Then she drowns in a shallow pond, even though she's a good swimmer, fit for her age and knows the area like the back of her hand, and no-one's even suspicious."

"Uh-oh." Susie groaned. "Is this another one of your hunches, Penny?"

Penny's eyes were blazing. "Don't you see? It's a clue from Mrs Montague. She left that card for me on purpose. What if she was scared and feared for her life, and that's why she was getting her affairs in order? After the Julia Wargraves murder case, I think Mrs Montague knew if she died in questionable circumstances, she could count on me to investigate. It's the least I can do, don't you think?" She handed the card to Susie and turned the key in the ignition, impatient to get back to Cherrytree Downs and pick Fischer up from her parents' house. The sooner she could start making inquiries, the better.

"It's also possible you're jumping to wild conclusions, and she put the card in the envelope by mistake." Susie folded the letter and put it back in the envelope along with the library card. She fastened her seat belt with a click as Penny drove out of the car park. “But something tells me you’re not going to let this go. Am I right?”

Penny gave her a sideways glance. “You know me too well. Maybe you’ll get your juicy story for the paper after all.”

Four

Edward Marshall, Penny's fiancé, shared Susie's lack of enthusiasm for the contents of the letter from Mrs Montague, although it wasn't hard to work out his reasons were more selfish. Susie simply wasn't interested in books, declaring she was lucky if she had time to read the texts on her phone. Edward, on the other hand, was used to spending his free time at the weekends with Penny. Depending on the time of year, that usually involved travelling to classic car shows in spring and summer, or something related to his vintage Mini restoration project the rest of the time. Whether it be going to collect parts he had ordered at on-line auction sites, or lovingly polishing the half-completed vehicle parked in the garage of his semi-detached home on the outskirts of Winstoke, he liked Penny to be by his side.

"It's hardly a princely sum for what could be a great deal of work," he said on Friday evening, when she told him how much she would be getting paid for sorting out the books at the manor. "Why didn't you agree an hourly rate with that Hawkins fellow? I can have a word with him, if you'd like. If this takes longer than you think, you'll be working for less than the minimum wage."

"Is money all you think about, Edward?"

"It's my job in case you've forgotten." He replied stiffly.

"And books are mine. Besides it's a lot to me," Penny replied, feeling defensive at his implication she was being taken advantage of. She had already decided to use the money for a trip to one of the International Literary Festivals she had not been to before, possibly Berlin. Of one thing she was sure, Edward would not be coming with her. She wasn't going to invite him, even though she was pretty certain he would decline anyway. "I'd have done it for free, and I told Mr Hawkins as much. Mrs Montague's entrusting of her family's library collection to me is an honour and something I take very seriously, and I have no intention of letting her down. I'm starting in the morning."

"But you'd let me down, when we've got things planned for the next few weekends." Edward's jaw was set. "I suppose this means you won't be able to go to the cinema next Tuesday night either?"

"There's no point speaking to you when you're like this." Penny gazed down to where Fischer, curled up in his bed in front of the fire, was staring at Edward with wary eyes. "It's only for a few weeks. Even Fischer thinks you're being unreasonable."

"Don't be ridiculous. Fischer is a *dog*, Penny. Dogs can't think."

"Well I can, and I think you're acting like a spoiled child. I've had enough of it. Maybe it will do us good to spend some time apart, doing things we both enjoy."

Edward's eyes narrowed. "What's that supposed to mean? You don't like spending time with me?"

Penny let Edward's argumentative mood wash over her. It wasn't worth bickering with someone who always had to have the last word. The truth was she was weary of accommodating Edward's whims, often at the expense of her own preference. Take, for example, the time he had known she really wanted to run the used book stall at the annual village Summer Fete, but insisted she make the trek all the way to Glasgow with him to look at Mini rally cars instead. Any time they went to the cinema, he always picked the movie, otherwise he was insufferable to sit beside. If it was a film he didn't like, Edward was that annoying person, checking his phone and getting up to go to the bathroom or the kiosk for more snacks. An art house film or anything subtitled was out of the question or she would have to put up with his moaning about it for days afterwards.

Penny had long before decided Edward was like a comfy old cardigan, safe and warm but not very exciting. She liked safe and warm as much as anyone, but a niggling thought at the back of her mind often came to the surface, declaring she deserved more. The safety aspect was still there, but the warmth had diminished considerably. Edward did tell her he loved her, but in such a way as though to remind her how lucky she was, and she expected their long engagement would end in marriage someday. However, not until Edward had been promoted to partner at his accountancy firm, one of his prerequisites before settling down.

When dealing with one of Edward's mini-rants, she found diplomacy the optimal solution. "I do like spending time with you," she answered, which was usually true. "But that doesn't mean we have to do everything together in our leisure time. And if we can't go to the cinema on Tuesday, we can go another night, surely?"

"Hmmph. Maybe."

Penny knew what that was about; Tuesday was the night for cheap tickets at Winstoke Cinema. Edward hated paying full price for anything, and insisted they share a giant tub of popcorn rather than having a small one each, because it was better value. The fact they never finished it was irrelevant.

"I'll make us dinner tomorrow night, and we can catch up over a bottle of wine. How does that sound? I can pick up a nice steak for you from the butcher's in the morning." Penny was a vegetarian, and cooking meat went against her personal views, she had used a meat substitute in the past and Edward hadn't known the difference. Edward's expression brightened. He stretched out his feet closer to the fire and lifted the remote control for the television. "That would be nice. Now, did you record that documentary for me?"

Penny had been going to ask him what he thought about

Mrs Montague leaving her library card in the envelope, as her suspicions of foul play had been questioned by Susie on the trip back to Cherrytree Downs that afternoon, as probably being a figment of Penny's overactive imagination, she wanted another opinion. But seeing how comfortable Edward looked, and a full blown argument thwarted, she decided to leave it. The chances of him agreeing with her were slim anyway.

She nodded. "Yes, I did. I'll put the kettle on."

Maybe she was being ridiculous, after all. Unless something came out of the woodwork, she should probably forget all about it.

Fischer's head twitched as the camper van made its way along the winding driveway to Cherrytree Manor, his nose pressed against the passenger window. The route inclined upwards towards the country house, an impressive Georgian residence which was only visible upon turning the final bend.

Originally surrounded by orchards and meadows which had been sold off over the years and now formed a large part of the village below, what acreage remained was occupied by a private garden with a wide lawn and mature hedges. Majestic old trees bordered the edge of the landscaped area, at the bottom of which was an ancient stone wishing well, fenced off to prevent accidents.

"Imagine living here, Fischer! You could get up to some mischief in that garden, I'm sure." Penny pulled the van to a standstill beside the weathered Land Rover that had been Mrs Montague's preferred mode of transport. There was a shiny Jaguar parked at the front of the house as well, but Penny couldn't remember ever having seen Mrs Montague driving it. She knew Celia Higgins, the housekeeper, sometimes used it to go to the supermarket in Winstoke, which wasn't often as Mrs Montague had liked to shop local.

Fischer began to pant and scratch at the door, eager to be let out to explore. Penny scooped him up and they climbed out. She didn't bother to lock the van, there was no need.

"When I was a little girl I used to think this place was something out of a fairy tale." It still looked magical, although not as big as it had seemed when she was only half the size. She set Fischer down as they approached the front door, which was behind a portico with four columns that had been added to the house when the front of the building was reconstructed after a fire. Heated by paraffin stoves and open hearths in those days, the threat of fire was an ever-present danger. The history of the house was well-documented, and Penny had researched it at the library while still at school. The site had been occupied for almost a thousand years since its original Saxon owner, with rebuilding having taken place at least three times.

The door creaked open before Penny had a chance to rap the solid brass knocker in the shape of a lion's head. Celia, wearing a housecoat, greeted them with a weak smile. Her eyes were red and watery.

"Hello, Penny. I was looking out for you. I'm glad you and Fischer are here. The place is so very… empty and quiet, without Mrs Montague." Her face crumpled, and Penny took a step closer.

"Oh, Celia. I'm so sorry. Is it all right for Fischer to come in? He is house-trained."

"Of course, dear, Mrs Montague adored the wee fellow, she wouldn't have minded at all. Follow me."

Penny had been inside the house on previous occasions at various charity events hosted by Mrs Montague, who was a generous patron of several causes, including the Summer Fete. However, those times she had been in one of the various reception rooms facing the garden. Now, Celia led her through the bowels of the house, along dim corridors and up and down various staircases, so that Penny lost her bearings completely. When they reached their destination, Penny found herself on a mezzanine overlooking what she could only describe as a gentleman's study.

"Mrs Montague didn't change a thing in here after her husband passed away," Celia said, her voice a proud whisper. "The newspaper's still on the desk from the day Mr Montague died, right beside his pipe." She jutted her chin out. "I dust regularly of course, but some of the shelves are too high for me to reach, and I don't like using the steps unless James, the gardener, holds them."

The faint aroma of old books in the room immediately made Penny feel at home. "Don't worry. I'll clean everything as I go along," she assured her.

"Mrs Montague liked to come and sit in here and read," Celia continued, looking around with a glassy gaze. She seemed in no hurry to leave. "You'll probably find her library books lying around, if she had any on loan."

"I'll keep an eye out for them." Penny felt a twinge of guilt for having assumed she wouldn't get them back.

Celia nodded to some cardboard boxes and tape on the floor. "I wasn't sure what you'd need, but I found some packing materials you can use. No doubt I'll have to get more, anyway, if the place is sold." She reached a hand into her pocket, pulling out a paper tissue. "Forgive me. It's all a bit much to take in. What with Master Milo and his entourage coming home for the funeral, all the beds need making up. Then they'll need feeding, no doubt." She blew into the tissue, making a trumpeting noise which caused Fischer to jump. "I'd best get on with it, I suppose. Let me know if you need anything."

"I will. Thanks, Celia."

Penny watched as Celia scurried out, Fischer hot on her heels. When the older woman realised she had a companion, she paused and bent down, her face breaking into a smile. "Do you want to come with me to the kitchen, Fischer? I think you can smell the pie I'm baking. Clever boy."

Reaching out to the nearest bookshelf, Penny gently ran

her fingers along the spines. She could tell some of the books were very old and would need careful handling. Others, not so much. Pulling out a paperback with a striking title, she looked at the illustrated cover that depicted the genre. It was a 1950's pulp fiction mystery, part of a long running series about a Californian private-eye. The series spanned three-dozen novels over forty years, during which the main character remained thirty years of age throughout. Smiling, she replaced the book and pulled out another.

When Fischer reappeared a while later, Penny had no idea how much time had passed, so engrossed had she been in discovering the delights that lay on the bookshelves surrounding her. As well as classics and historical treasures, she had found Mr Montague's PhD thesis, as well as celebrity biographies and several trashy romances. And that was only one small section of the shelves which stretched all the way to the ceiling. What she loved about the collection was that it was real, there was no snobbery, or question of books being displayed just for show. They had been read and enjoyed, regardless of their artistic merit.

"Get off those books, little man, they're not for climbing on." Penny shooed Fischer away and straightened up from where she had been kneeling on the floor in the midst of several piles she had started to categorise. Her knees creaked, and she found she had pins and needles in both feet. Wincing, she shook out each leg in turn and massaged her calves until the blood began to flow again.

The chinking of china made her turn around. Celia had entered, carrying a tray. "I've brought you some tea and sandwiches, Penny. Fischer and I have already eaten, and Fischer's had a run outside, although I'll join you for a cup of tea, if I may? I believe you're somewhat of a tea connoisseur, and Mrs Montague kept quite a collection. Lapsang Souchong all right? It has a rather nice smoky pine flavour which I thought you'd enjoy."

She set the tray on the desk of the study, and Penny came down the steps from the mezzanine. As well as the china cups and teapot, there was a selection of finger sandwiches made with soft white bread with the crusts cut off.

"No meat, I know you don't eat it," Celia added. "I remembered from the Christmas dinner in the Village Hall, when you had the vegetarian option."

Penny was touched. "You didn't have to go to all this trouble, Celia, but thank you. I'll just go and wash my hands first. I found one of Mrs Montague's library books, by the way, so I'm sure the others are here somewhere."

"That's good, dear. The nearest bathroom's just down the hall. Second on the right after the watercolour of Winstoke Castle."

Myrtle's housekeeper was much chirpier than she had been earlier in the day, and Penny paused, wondering whether to risk asking her the burning question. It had been weighing on her mind, but she feared upsetting her again.

Celia made the decision for her. "What is it, dear?"

"Mrs Montague left me her library card in the envelope containing the letter she gave to her solicitor last week. I've been worried about what it means, and was wondering if you might have any idea?"

Not even a flicker of surprise registered on Celia's face at this turn of events. "It means she feared she was going to die, of course. What else could it be?"

Five

"'That man will be the death of me.' Those were her exact words." Celia's expression was deadly serious. "And here we are, not a week later, and poor Mrs Montague's gone. What do you make of that?" The china teacups and saucers rattled as she laid them on top of the gold-leaf-embossed leather inserted in the antique wooden desk, along with silver spoons on each saucer. As well as the sandwiches and a side plate for Penny, she placed a small bowl of sugar cubes and a jug of milk in the centre, before looking up.

Penny was staring at her, open-mouthed. "Mrs Montague said that? When was this, Celia?"

Celia nodded, and tilted her head to the side, thinking for a moment or two. "Last weekend. It was Saturday night, I remember because we were watching the celebrity ballroom dancing show on television." A faint smile crossed her face. "She telephoned, to cast a vote for the newsreader with two left feet. But they got voted out in the dance-off. We didn't usually watch television together, except for that one show if we were both at home. I don't think I'll be able to face it tonight." She swallowed, rummaging for her tissue again.

"Who was she talking about, did she say?"

"That dreadful man next door, I expect. Nick Staines. Do you know him?"

"Not really. I've just seen him around. He's hard to miss, in that car of his." Penny couldn't remember the name of the expensive brand of vehicle that Nick drove, although Edward had explained to her, in revered tones, it was the Holy Grail of sports cars apparently. All she knew was, it was very loud, and Nick drove it like he was in a Grand Prix. The fact that anyone would choose to buy a car costing more than some people's houses was beyond her, no matter how much money they had to spare. She could think of plenty of ways it could be put to better use, for the wider good.

Celia wiped her sniffles away and dragged another chair over to the desk. "Off you go to the bathroom, dear. I'll pour the tea."

"Thank you." Penny headed for the door. When Fischer made a move to follow her, Penny shook her head. "I'll be back in a minute, Fischer. You stay here with Celia." He stared at her, ears cocked, before obediently trotting back to the desk, where Celia was waiting with a home-made dog treat and a hug.

As she wandered down the hallway, Penny's mind was in a whirl. The interior of the part of the house she found herself in was grand, but not as formal as the reception rooms Mrs Montague had used for entertaining. The walls were painted in a duck-egg blue, and chintz curtains with swags and tails draped the full-length windows. Outside, she could see the gardener driving a golf buggy across the lawn, laden with tools of the trade. Spotting the watercolour painting of Winstoke Castle, moments later she was freshening up in a small traditional bathroom wallpapered in Toile de Joie.

Penny considered what she knew about Nick Staines. Early forties, she guessed, although there had been debate about his age in the village. Some said his youthful looks weren't natural and were enhanced by non-surgical procedures. Whether or not that was true she had no idea, but if not, he had either been blessed with good genes or the years had been kind to him. His line of work was something vague, but media-related. As far as anyone could tell it seemed to involve socialising with celebrities in London and having his photograph taken for tabloid newspapers with scantily-clad models. One of the fast set who zoomed around Hampsworthy Downs, she wasn't sure why he had been so keen to buy the land and build an imposing modern home on it in the first place. By all accounts, he was away more often than he was in residence. What, she wondered, had he done to upset Mrs Montague?

Celia was dabbing her eyes when Penny returned. "Don't mind me. You eat your lunch, dear." She pushed the sandwiches towards Penny. "There's egg and watercress, cream cheese and celery, and cucumber and tomato. I hope you like them."

"You shouldn't have gone to so much trouble. I hope it didn't delay you from all your other jobs? I know you have a lot to do."

Penny selected a finger sandwich, demolishing it in two bites. They were dainty, and she was hungry. She had planned to go home for lunch, but it would have been rude to refuse after Celia had made them. "Mm, these are delicious. Thank you."

"You're welcome." Celia opened her mouth to say something else, then stopped.

"Tell me about Nick Staines," Penny said cautiously, taking a sip of her tea. "Why do you think Mrs Montague said what she did?"

"He was here, last Saturday afternoon." Celia was hesitant. "I wasn't eavesdropping, but there were raised voices. I couldn't help overhearing."

"Of course." Penny was solemn. "Go on."

"There had been one of his parties the night before, and the music was very loud. Some of the guests were out the back, smoking, so those big glass doors of his were open into the garden. The sound carries you know."

"I'm sure it does." It was quiet up on the hill, there being no through road across the Downs. Nick's house was on the other side of the trees, and whilst it was shielded from direct view of the manor, it wasn't actually far away as the crow flies.

"Mrs Montague told me the following morning she had rapped on his front door before breakfast to have a word.

A half-naked woman came to the door wearing nothing but a man's shirt and told her Nick was still in bed." Celia gave an exaggerated eye-roll. "Can you imagine? The trollop would have had a piece of my tongue, but I expect Myrtle was far too polite."

Penny suppressed a smile. Somehow, she didn't think anything would have shocked Mrs Montague.

Celia, it appeared, was just getting into her stride. It all came tumbling out, how Nick had come around to the manor later that afternoon, and accused Myrtle of being, amongst other things, 'a crabby old witch.' Myrtle had held her own, giving him short shrift about being rude to her in her own home. "Said she was all for people having fun, and if he'd had the courtesy to warn us beforehand, we could have bought earplugs," Celia added. "And then he had the cheek to say she should sell up, preferably to him, and move away, if she didn't like it. Quite belligerent, he was, too."

"That's awful. What did Mrs Montague do?"

"She asked him to leave and said she would call PC Bolton if he didn't go quietly. Not that old Humphrey Bolton's much use, if you ask me. Ever since he announced his upcoming retirement he seems to have gone to ground. You'll find him in the Pig and Fiddle, more often than not. Sooner he hangs up his boots and they get someone worth their salt in the police house, the better."

"Oh dear." Penny didn't want to say anything negative about PC Bolton, who lived in the police house in the village, but privately she thought Celia was right. He had been of little help when one of the villagers had been murdered a short while before, and it had been her and Mr Kelly who had ended up working with Detective Inspector Monroe to solve the case instead.

"It's not the first time Nick Staines upset her, either." Celia pursed her lips. "She may have stood up to him when he was here, but she was quite flustered when he'd gone. I had to pour her a stiff drink. Every time he's been home, there's been something. If you want my opinion, he was wearing her down until she'd had enough, and agreed to his offer to buy the place."

"I knew they didn't get along, but I had no idea things were so bad." *Bad enough to kill her, and be done with it?* From what Celia was saying, Penny thought it sounded like Mrs Montague had no intention of caving in to Nick's demands. A woman in her seventies, in good health, before the incident at the duck pond, her life expectancy was probably good. *Maybe Nick ran out of patience.*

There was something else Penny didn't understand. "Why does he want this place so badly, anyway? I mean, it's very imposing, of course, but I didn't think it would be Nick's style."

"Luxury apartments," Celia said with a knowing look, her eyes wide. "Mr Jebb at the Planning Office told Mrs Montague he received a preliminary enquiry for an agreement in principle to build apartments on part of Nick's land next door. Had she been alive, Mrs Montague would have objected to any formal planning application, of course."

"Ah, that makes more sense." Penny was starting to see the bigger picture. If Nick owned Mrs Montague's land, not only would there be no-one to object to new apartments on Nick's property, he would be free to develop the rest of the land as well. She was aware of other stately homes further afield that had been converted into apartments and sold for prices way beyond the reach of most local residents of The Downs. If she were a betting person, she would have wagered that the people in Nick's circle were just the sort who would snap them up.

"More tea, Celia?" She reached for the teapot and topped up Celia's cup. The longer she could keep her talking and the more background information she could garner, the better.

"Thank you, Penny. Mrs Montague told me her solicitor was dealing with it, that's all I know." Celia added a drop of milk to her teacup, and a sugar lump, before stirring.

Thinking back to her meeting with Mr Hawkins, Penny had not got any indication he thought there was anything untoward about Myrtle's death. "Celia, this is important. Did Mrs Montague ever say that Nick had threatened her, or anything like that? I realise it's a serious allegation, and I don't want to put words in your mouth, but I'm just wondering if he crossed a line."

Celia sighed. "Not that I know of. He's a bully, I saw

and heard that for myself. If there was anything more to it, I don't think Myrtle would have shared it with me in any case. She was my employer after all, although we got on very well. I thought the world of her." Her eyes welled up again. "I can't help blaming myself. If I'd raised the alarm sooner, maybe she could have been saved."

"There's nothing you could have done." Penny reached over and squeezed Celia's hand, the remaining sandwiches forgotten about. "Don't even think that. I'm sure Mrs Montague wouldn't want you to."

"I wasn't home until after ten that evening. I'd been at the cinema with my sister to see the Hollywood musical everyone's been talking about," Celia went on, choking back a sob. "I locked the door, thinking Myrtle was already home from her walk. I didn't hear her make her cocoa for bed, but then I don't always. My rooms are on the other side of the house, so unless I'm downstairs I wouldn't." Her eyes implored Penny. "Why didn't I check if she was home? I keep asking myself that, over and over."

"Ssh, you mustn't think that," Penny soothed. "There's nothing anyone could have done." Another thought occurred to her. "I saw Mrs Montague on her way to The Pig and Fiddle, and she said she was meeting someone later that evening. Did she mention to you who it was, by any chance?"

Celia shook her head. "No, not a word, just that I shouldn't make dinner as she was eating out. Do you think you and Fischer can help find out who killed her, the way you did with Julia Wargraves' murder? I do hope so, so she can rest in peace."

Fischer whined at the sound of his name, and Penny gave Celia a sad smile. "We don't know for sure if anyone did kill her," she whispered. "But rest assured, Celia, I'm going to make it a priority to find out."

Six

Penny peered around the door of the kitchen, and saw Celia washing pots and pans, her arms elbow-deep in a sink of soapy water. "I'm going to call it a day, Celia, but I'll be back on Monday evening, if that's all right?"

Celia turned and smiled. "How did you get on?"

"I made a good start." Penny was pleased with her progress, having catalogued several rows of books, and sorted them into piles. There was one for the library van, another for the local schools and Further Education college in Winstoke, and the smallest pile contained several first editions and collector's items she thought may be of interest to the British Library. Their policy on potential donations meant she would need to contact them to check if the items were a good fit with their collection. And sometimes, conservation and storage costs meant that they declined offers even when it was material they did not hold.

"You come back any time, my dear. You're no trouble and Fischer's a delight to have around the place. I'm expecting Master Milo will have arrived by Monday, but I'm sure you won't be in his way either. You're carrying out his mother's wishes, after all." Celia pulled her hands out of the sink and wiped them on a towel. "Any plans for tonight? I hope Edward is taking you somewhere nice."

"I'm cooking him dinner." Almost as though she was apologising for Edward, Penny added, "We don't go out much."

Celia tutted. "Lovely woman like you, deserves to be treated like a queen. I hope he knows that."

"I think he needs a reminder. I'll tell him you said so. Bye, Celia."

Celia's words had struck a chord, and on the way to the van, Penny mulled them over. It wasn't that she was unhappy in her relationship with Edward, but they were stuck in a bit of a rut. An ambitious man, it seemed to her as though he gave his work his all, and there wasn't much left for her. She loved her job too, but she didn't prioritise it over the people she cared for the most. Which was why she needed to hurry, if she was to get to Winstoke and back before Edward arrived.

Darkness was falling, and her pace quickened. It was a grey, damp afternoon, dreech, as her Scottish grandmother would have said. As a child, Penny had spent many happy summer holidays with her on the Isle of Bute when she was alive, and remembered the local terms with fondness.

Fischer, running ahead, let out a sharp yelp as she approached the van, fumbling in her bag for her keys.

"What the… " A silhouette appeared from nowhere, startling Penny. "Stupid mutt," the man said, raising his foot in the direction of Fischer's tail.

"Hey! Don't you dare!" she shouted, just in time for Fischer to dart out of the way. "Stop that. What do you think you're doing?"

James, the gardener, faced her with a scowl. "Thought it was going to bite me. Didn't see you there. You should have him on a lead." He stomped off, muttering under his breath, leaving Penny to stare after him in shocked surprise.

She scooped Fischer up and carried him the rest of the way to the van, stroking his fur. "Are you okay, Fish Face? Don't listen to that horrible man, and if you see him again, stay out of his way. Got it?"

Fischer let out a tiny whine in response.

They climbed in. "I'm just going to call ahead to the Police Station, Fischer, and let them know we're coming." She scrolled through the list of contacts on her phone. Inspector Monroe's mobile phone number was saved on the device from their previous investigation, and she considered calling him direct, but plumped for contacting the switchboard to start with. "If Inspector Monroe's not at the station, then I'll call his mobile. How does that sound?" She looked across at Fischer, who was staring at her with wide eyes and a cheeky grin. "Good, I'm glad you agree."

"Ah, there you are. I thought you'd changed your mind about coming." Inspector Monroe was standing at the front desk of the police station when Penny rushed in, soaking wet, carrying a bedraggled Fischer. "I'm glad I waited an extra five minutes."

Penny grimaced. "Sorry. The traffic was mayhem. Saturday afternoon shoppers, and then the downpour…"

Inspector Monroe's smile reached his eyes. There was no hint of irritation or impatience at her having taken thirty minutes longer to get there than she had expected. "Don't apologise. It's always great to see you, Penny. And Fischer too, of course. Come on through." He led them down the corridor to an interview room, warmed by overhead heaters. Fischer was wriggling in Penny's arms, trying to break free.

"I'm going to set him down now," she warned the Inspector when they were inside the room. "You might want to stand back."

They waited while Fischer shook the water off his coat, and then ran up to Inspector Monroe, rubbing against his ankles.

"I think he likes you," Penny said.

Inspector Monroe grinned down at Fischer before looking back at Penny. "The feeling's mutual. You should get your wet coat off as well, or you'll catch a cold."

Penny did so, and the Inspector pulled out a chair for

her. He sat facing her across the desk, an unopened notebook and a pen beside him on the table, and her stomach flipped. She had forgotten quite how handsome he was. Her eyes were drawn to his strong hands, rugged in comparison to Edward's manicured ones.

Inspector Monroe gazed at her in concern. "Is everything okay, Penny? I was worried in case you're in some kind of trouble."

Penny took a deep breath, and it all came tumbling out.

Inspector Monroe listened while Penny outlined her suspicions, taking notes and asking questions for clarification, and nodding his head now and then as she spoke.

"Well?" Penny was breathless by the time she had finished. "Do you see why I think Mrs Montague's death wasn't an accident?"

"Hmm." The Inspector was non-committal, rubbing his chin. He scanned his notes again before addressing Penny. "Let me check I've got this straight. You think Mrs Montague may have been murdered because she was a good swimmer and also because of what Celia told you about Nick Staines. Is that right?"

"Yes." It had taken Penny a lot longer to explain what the Inspector had just summarised in a couple of sentences. It didn't sound quite so sinister when he said it. "And the library card, remember? I think Myrtle wanted me to investigate if her fears were realised and something happened to her. As Celia said, the timing of her death was very close to the incident last week with Nick Staines."

The Inspector didn't look convinced. If anything, she got the impression he was humouring her. The patient smile painted on his face was a giveaway. "I see. And, you want the police to investigate the incident further? Interview Celia Higgins and also speak to the neighbour, Nick Staines, is that correct?"

Penny nodded.

"I'm not at liberty to discuss the case," he replied at last. "It appears to have been a tragic accident. However, you know yourself that nothing can be ruled out until we have the results of the autopsy. The coroner's report should be available at the start of the week. In the meantime, I have a few thoughts, if you'd like to hear them."

"Go on." This wasn't going the way Penny had hoped.

"I'm not sure that Mrs Montague's swimming ability or otherwise has a great deal of bearing, people have been known to drown in only a few inches of water, particularly if they have lost consciousness for any reason. It's slippery around the duck pond in this weather, and it's quite likely that if Mrs Montague slipped, she also hurt herself some way, either before or after submersion. An injury could have limited her swimming capability. The water was very cold, and the temperature was around freezing on the night in question. No one could have sustained a long period of time in the pond in those conditions, especially a woman of advancing years with very little body fat."

With reluctance, Penny agreed.

"Regarding Mr Staines," the Inspector continued, "his calling Mrs Montague names was vulgar, but it doesn't necessarily make him a suspect in her death."

"What about Mrs Montague saying he would be the death of her? Does that not count for something?"

The Inspector sighed. "You said Celia assumed Mrs Montague was talking about Mr Staines when she made that comment, but there's no definitive proof that's who she was referring to. It's also a common phrase, which most people don't mean in the literal sense."

Penny bit her lip, trying to maintain her composure. Her hopes of finding an ally in Inspector Monroe were being dashed by the second. Not only that, she was beginning to feel foolish for having made such a fuss about insisting to speak to him urgently. For all she knew, she had kept him late for something important. Instead, here she was, wasting police time. "Why would she have left me the library card, in that case?" She was mumbling now, and realised herself she was clutching at straws.

"I have no answer to that one, except to say if Mrs Montague thought she was in danger, why didn't she raise it with someone who could have helped her while she was still alive? It seems bizarre for her to wait until after her death to raise the alarm, if that was indeed the intention."

There it was. Game, set and match to the Inspector. Not that he was trying to humiliate her, Penny was sure. His expression was still kind, his eyes soft, but his graciousness made her feel worse. Thoroughly embarrassed, she had an urge to get out of there as quickly as possible.

"You're probably right," she murmured. "I won't take up any more of your time, Inspector. Please excuse me if I've acted out of turn. It's just that Mrs Montague was such a nice old lady, and if she was the victim of foul play I'd like to see justice done on her behalf. I just thought it better to make you aware of everything, that's all."

"Absolutely, that was the right course of action and I appreciate it. I'll let you know if there's anything else you can do to help us."

Standing, Penny pulled her coat from the back of the chair and slipped her arms through the still-wet sleeves. "Come on, Fischer, time to go."

Inspector Monroe walked them to the front door of the building. "Thanks for coming in, Penny. I'm glad you did. Enjoy the rest of your weekend."

"You too," she said, her cheeks flaming.

"Where have you been? I've been trying to get hold of you for the last hour." Edward sounded irate. "Did you not get my messages to call me?"

"Yes, I did. All five of them. I left my phone in the van, and I've just got back to the car park now." She was still smarting from the embarrassing experience at the police station and didn't feel like sharing it with him. "What's wrong, is it an emergency?"

"Something has come up at work. I'm at the office now. I just wanted to let you know I'll be late and not to put my steak on until I get to your place. I can't eat it if it's not pink."

Penny silently counted to three before replying. She had run back to the van to try and get home quicker, and it transpired she needn't have bothered. Brightening, she remembered what Celia had said about Edward taking her out somewhere and had an idea. "Why don't I meet you in Winstoke later when you're finished? I can get ready and leave Fischer with my parents. Then you don't have to rush. We could try the new French bistro."

"No need, if you're cooking, Penny. You can always take me to the French bistro for my birthday."

Something inside Penny snapped. For her last birthday, Edward had given her an egg-timer and a box of chocolates. "Actually, let's leave it tonight, Edward. I'll talk to you tomorrow, okay?" She could hear him splutter at the other end of the line, and she winked at Fischer, who was perched on her knee.

"Is something wrong? What have I done now?"

"Nothing, Edward." Nothing. That was precisely the point. "Good night."

Seven

Penny squinted in the early morning darkness, still groggy from just having woken up. Patting the wall to find the light switch beside the door, she peered at the empty dog bed beside the hearth.

"Fischer, where are you?"

She looked around the living room, but he was nowhere to be seen.

"Is this some kind of game? Do you need to go out? Don't worry, I'm coming now."

Walking through the archway into the kitchen, she expected to see Fischer waiting by the back door to be let out into the small garden, but there was no sign of him there either. A low growl from the hallway startled her, and she paused to listen.

"Fischer?"

There it was again, then a series of barks, which caused Penny to spin on her heels and rush back the way she had come. She found the little terrier at the end of the hallway, still yapping.

"Ssh. This isn't like you, Fish Face, what is it?"

At the sight of Penny, Fischer pawed the mat and emitted a soft whine.

"What's that?"

She drew closer, it was only a piece of paper.

"It's okay, Fischer. Someone's just dropped something through the door. It's probably a leaflet for something or other. I'll get it later. Come on, it's time for breakfast."

It vaguely occurred to Penny that whoever had put it through the letterbox must have been out either very early that morning, or late the previous night. There had been nothing there when she locked up the night before, and who delivered promotional leaflets at the crack of dawn on a Sunday?

Fischer barked again.

"Fine, have it your way." Penny crouched down to pick up the paper. Puzzled, she saw it was a lined white page that had been torn from a notebook. Straightening up, she unfolded it, and read words which set her heart pounding.

STOP POKING AROUND IN THINGS THAT DON'T CONCERN YOU OR YOU'LL BE SORRY.

Handwritten in blue ballpoint pen in slanted capitals, Penny was not surprised to see the note was unsigned.

She gazed down at Fischer, the paper fluttering in her trembling hand. "No wonder you were upset, Fischer. Clever boy! You know what this means, don't you? We must be on to something."

"Blimey!" Susie's mouth gaped when she read the note. "This is scary stuff. Have you called the police?"

"Not yet. I came straight here after Fischer and I finished our walk. I hope you don't mind. I didn't want to wake my parents, and they'd worry too much anyway."

Susie munched her toast. "So, you thought you'd wake me up instead?"

"Nice try. You were already up, the lights were on," Penny said.

"Yes, I know. The kids are going to their dad's. Speaking of which, he'll be here soon." Susie got up and walked to the window, opening it before calling to her children who were playing outside with Fischer. "Billy, Ellen, have you got your things? Ellen, don't spin around like that when you're holding Fischer. He'll get dizzy and sick. You will as well, come to think of it." She walked back to the kitchen table and sat down. "By the way, aren't you forgetting someone?"

Penny sipped her tea, ignoring Susie's question.

"Stop pretending you didn't hear me, Miss Finch." Susie lifted the note again and waved it under Penny's nose. "What does Edward make of this?"

"He doesn't know anything about it."

"Why not?"

"I haven't told him yet." Penny avoided eye-contact with Susie. She knew Edward was not her friend's favourite person. Not that Susie had ever said anything bad about him, but she didn't have to. "We had a slight falling out."

"I'm sorry he upset you, but I'm not sorry you stood up to him," Susie said, once Penny finished explaining what had happened. "Good for you. It will do him no harm to stew for a while."

"That's what I thought." Penny gave her a rueful smile. "I'm still mad at him, but he probably won't understand why. He was just being his usual selfish self. And because I've always tolerated his behaviour, he won't see why it's unacceptable."

Susie raised an eyebrow. "Don't let him off the hook that easily, Penny. Explain how it makes you feel when he treats you like that."

"I'll talk to him properly later to clear the air."

"Good, then he can show you how much he loves you by protecting you from whoever wrote this creepy note." Seeing the worry etched on Penny's face, Susie added, "Until the person's found, of course. Which they will be. Very soon."

Penny twisted a strand of her hair, something she always did when she was nervous. "Easy for you to say. I don't relish the thought of being the next victim. Whoever wrote the note must be Myrtle's killer, and now they're after me. What I don't understand is, how does the person know I was poking around at all, as they put it? Of the people I've discussed it with, you and Inspector Monroe both nicely told me I was imagining things. And I doubt Celia's the killer, so she must have mentioned our conversation to somebody else."

Susie's face fell. "Oh dear. I think that might have been me."

Penny groaned. "Go on."

"After I went to the solicitor's office with you for that meeting, my boss asked me about it when I got back to work on Friday. He wanted to know how the piece on Mrs Montague was coming along. I joked if you had your way it would be another story of small-town murder and intrigue. I said if there was any mileage in that angle, we could count on you to deliver the scoop, and the murderer."

"Need I remind you, your boss is probably the biggest loudmouth in The Downs?" As the editor of the Gazette, it was Archie Cryer's business to know everyone else's. Stirring the pot was how he ensured a never-ending stream of stories for the paper. "There won't be a soul who doesn't know I'm up to my neck in this by now."

Susie chewed her lip. "I'm so sorry, Penny. I never thought for a minute anything like this would happen."

"I know. Don't worry, it's not your fault." Penny's brow was creased. "All the more people to look out for me, hopefully."

"Absolutely, that's the spirit." Susie swung into action, or as Penny called it, mum mode. "First things first. When Billy and Ellen have gone, I'll come to the police station with you, and they can make a start on getting this lunatic off the streets. How does that sound?"

Penny mustered a smile. "Perfect. Could we go in your car? I don't want to take the van just in case it's been tampered with." She had visions of the brakes not working and careering into the tree on the bend at the bottom of Sugar Hill. "Edward's the very person to take a look at it later."

"Crikey! What an awful thought. Of course I'll drive. Hang on, there's the doorbell." Susie jumped up and rapped on the window pane again, gesturing for Billy and Ellen to come in. "Let me sort out the children and then we'll go."

Susie pulled the car to a stop outside Penny's house.

"Won't be a moment," Penny said, opening her door. "Stay here with Fischer. I'll just get my bag." A thought occurred to her. "Actually, you'd better come in. I could probably do with making myself slightly more presentable. They might take me a bit more seriously at the police station if my hair is combed, for starters. I came out this morning with a lick and a promise."

Susie switched off the engine. "That's understandable, in the circumstances." She glanced across at Penny and grinned. "But from what you've told me about your meeting with Inspector Monroe yesterday, I agree taming your hair is a good idea, if you want to add gravitas to the proceedings. Otherwise it makes you look a bit… scatty or something."

"Nice choice of words. I'll take scatty. Left to its own

devices, my hair could be described as a lot worse. Come on then, I might need your help."

Inside, Susie wandered into the living room, while Penny went upstairs. Fischer, spoilt for choice as to which one to follow, plumped for Penny, and trotted along behind her.

In her bedroom, Penny yanked off the baggy old sweatshirt she was wearing and replaced it with a chunky mustard knit. Her jeans were respectable, but even more so when she swapped her trainers for a pair of ankle boots she pulled out from under the bed.

Straightening up, she checked herself in the mirror. "What do you think, Fischer? Is that better?" She wanted to look nice, for the sake of her own confidence as much as anything, although perhaps there was an underlying reason she wasn't quite ready to accept. And anyway, Inspector Monroe might not even be there.

Fischer, sitting in the doorway of her bedroom, woofed.

"Thank you, Little Man."

Humming to herself, she sat at the dressing table and rooted through a small cosmetics bag, the contents of which she rarely used. Using a plump brush, she swept a hint of blusher across her pale cheeks to give them a warm glow. A sparing application of concealer served to hide the shadows under her blue eyes, and a couple of coats of mascara made them pop. Liking what she saw, she decided a subtle lipstick wouldn't hurt either.

Her messy mop of hair was more of a challenge. When

it was blow-dried, it was fairly presentable, but not having washed it that morning it was sticking up all over the place, and she looked as though she'd had a fight with a hedge, in a wind tunnel. In the end, she settled for tearing a comb through it, wincing as she did so.

"That's the best I can do, Fischer. Let's go, or Susie will be wondering where we've got to."

Downstairs, Susie was leafing through one of the books on the coffee table. She addressed Penny without lifting her head. "Is this book any good? It says it's a psychological thriller about an agoraphobic woman who spies on her neighbours and thinks she sees a crime. I've to write a book review for the paper, so if I'm going to have to actually read something it may as well be enjoyable."

"You make it sound as though reading is torture. It really isn't, you know. That book's pretty good, but if you don't have time to read it, I'll write a review for you to publish. No charge. Call it a thank you for being my bodyguard for the morning."

"You've got yourself a deal." Susie looked up, and her eyes widened. "Are you wearing make up? It suits you." She grinned, "Anything you want to tell me?"

"I've no idea what you mean," Penny said, her natural colour rising. "Aren't you the one who always says a little bit of makeup makes you feel ready to take on the world? It's not every day my life gets threatened, so I thought I'd give it a try, that's all."

Susie chuckled. "In that case, we should finish what you've started. That hair of yours needs sorting out. Do you still have the hot irons from the ill-fated hair straightening episode?"

"Ha ha. I thought we weren't going to mention that ever again."

"We're not, I promise. Just go and get them, and I'll show you a trick. You can thank me afterwards."

Grumbling, Penny did as she was told. After ten minutes of primping and twisting, Susie declared she was done. She stood back to admire her handiwork. "Perfect. You can go and take a look now."

Staring into the hallway mirror, Penny gasped when she saw her reflection. "Is that me? How did you do that?" Bouncy waves grazed her shoulders, in a messy-but-done look. Rather than random strands sticking out at all angles, kinks were strategically placed. Best of all, the halo of frizz had gone, thanks to a tiny drop of the hair oil Susie carried around in her bag.

Susie and Fischer joined her in the hallway. "I'll show you another time. It just takes a little practice. Ready?"

Penny nodded. "As I'll ever be."

"Now do you believe that Mrs Montague was murdered? and the killer is coming after me?" Penny was once again sitting opposite Inspector Monroe in the interview room at Winstoke Police Station. Fischer, too, had made himself at home underneath the table.

The Inspector, it seemed, was never off duty. Unshaven, with shirt sleeves rolled up to show muscular forearms, and dark hair falling across his forehead as he inspected the note Penny had brought, he looked as though he'd been there all night. "I can't comment as to the possibility of murder, but I can assure you, we will be taking this note very seriously, Penny. Your safety is of paramount importance. While we're investigating, I'll have one of my officers check in on you a couple of times a day to make sure you're okay."

"PC Bolton?" Penny's heart sank. She rearranged her face, hoping her disappointment didn't show. PC Bolton was an elderly, pleasant, bumbling sort of policeman, more suited to giving directions and helping pedestrians across roads than protecting people from murderers. The problem was, Inspector Monroe still wasn't convinced there *was* a murderer.

"I'll see what I can do. If I can send someone who is more experienced I will certainly try and do so. I'll keep this, if that's all right with you?" With gloved hands, he slipped the note into a plastic cover, sealed it, and scribbled something on the label.

"Of course." Penny realised there was nothing else she could do. Deflated, she inhaled sharply, trying to hold herself together. The rush of adrenalin she had felt earlier had deserted her. Breaking down in tears wasn't going to achieve anything, apart from upsetting Fischer and embarrassing herself. "Thank you."

"Do you need a lift home or anything? I'm just about to finish my shift. Or rather, it's yesterday's shift. I never quite made it out the door. Something else came up after you were here."

"Thanks, but it's fine. Susie's waiting."

Monroe's expression flickered. If he wondered why Edward had not accompanied her on her visit, he never commented. Instead, he stood up, and walking to the door held it open for her.

In the hallway, he hesitated, gazing at her for a moment longer than was comfortable. "You look different today, Penny. You seem… " He took a step closer, looking into Penny's eyes, transfixed. She caught her breath and their surroundings seem to fade away.

"Sorry, lack of sleep," he murmured, shaking his head. "Please, keep in touch. If there's anything else at all, call me on my direct line, day or night."

"I will, thanks." Penny walked slowly back to Susie, her legs like jelly.

"Outside, quick, for the debrief," Susie hissed, when Penny and Fischer reached the end of the hallway where it opened into the waiting area.

On the way back to the car, Penny brought Susie up to speed on the meeting with the Inspector. She ended with a sigh, "As far as convincing him of Mrs Montague's murder, he's not interested. Although, he was reassuring about the note and said they would do their best to get to the bottom of it."

"You missed a bit." Susie raised an eyebrow. "You know, when DI Monroe gave you that smouldering look as you were leaving? I saw it all. He was definitely admiring you. For a second, I thought he was going to lean in and kiss you."

Penny hoped Susie couldn't hear her heart pounding through her chest. "Don't be ridiculous. You watch too many soap operas." She turned on the car radio to distract Susie from asking any more questions, secretly pleased her imagination had not been playing tricks on her.

Eight

"Looks like it's just you and me, Fischer."

Penny fastened the door chain on the inside of the door and pushed down the snib to secure the lock. A legacy from the cottage's previous owners, the chain allowed the door to be opened slightly to identify visitors. She'd never had reason to use it but considered it wouldn't do any harm as a precaution. As safety features went, it offered scant protection from intruders, but it provided her with some peace of mind. If there were ever uninvited guests it should buy her a little time.

She leaned the golf club Susie had given her against the wall behind the door. It belonged to Susie's son, Billy, and accepting it was the only way Susie would let her go back into the house alone.

"Here," Susie had said, after explaining she had to get something out of the boot of the car when she dropped Penny home. "It's a driver. Billy won't be playing golf again until spring. He won't miss it."

"I know what it is." Penny waved it away. "I don't want it.

If I hit someone with that thing, it will be me going to jail."

Susie placed a hand on her hip. "I didn't say you had to use it. Think of it as a deterrent."

"I became quite proficient in my self defense classes at university, remember? It might be a while since I've practised, but I'm quite sure if I'm threatened I'll remember the moves."

"I don't care. I'm not leaving unless you take it."

In the end Penny had accepted the club with a sigh. She knew that look of determination on Susie's face. "Anything for a quiet life. Thanks." Only then had Susie driven away, promising to telephone her regularly throughout the afternoon to make sure she was safe.

Door secured, Penny wandered into the living room and let out an involuntary shiver. In her hurry to get away earlier she had not banked up the fire, and it had gone out. She rubbed her hands together. "Let's get warmed up, Fischer. Then we'll get some lunch. Moping around isn't going to achieve anything."

Sorting out the fire was nothing a fire-lighter and some kindling couldn't fix, and by the time Penny and Fischer had eaten, the living room was once again toasty. Mug of tea in hand, she sank into the cushions on the sofa. Moments later, Fischer jumped up to join her. Curled on her lap, she stroked him with her free hand. Note or no note, she knew she was going to be okay, if only because of her inner conviction that whatever life threw at her, she could deal with it.

The moment was broken by a series of loud knocks on the door, and a voice calling through the letterbox. "Penny? Open up, it's me."

Fischer cocked his head, then nestled back down again.

Penny smiled, nudging him so she could get up. "It's Edward, Fischer. We can't just ignore him."

She opened the door to a sheepish-looking Edward, who was carrying a plastic bag and a bunch of drooping service station flowers. "I come in peace," he smiled, offering her the flowers. "Sorry about last night."

"Me too." Penny said, accepting the bouquet and standing back to let him in.

He placed his hand in the small of her back and gave her a fleeting kiss. "Hey," he said, catching her eye. He gently tilted her face up towards him. "What's wrong?"

To her surprise, Penny's eyes were welling with tears, and she choked back a sob. "Let me put the flowers in water, I've got quite a lot to tell you."

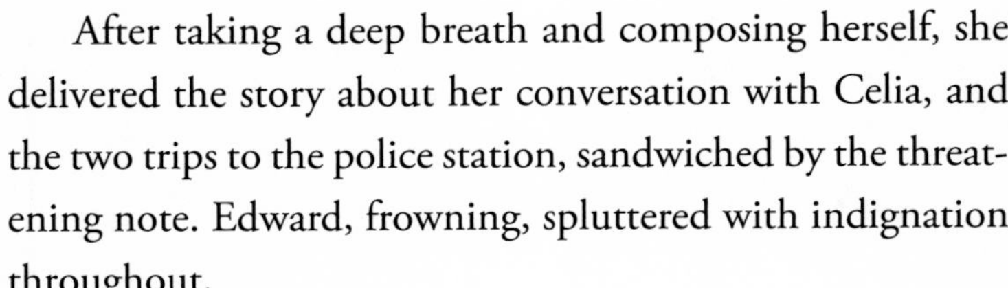

After taking a deep breath and composing herself, she delivered the story about her conversation with Celia, and the two trips to the police station, sandwiched by the threatening note. Edward, frowning, spluttered with indignation throughout.

"So, there you have it. What do you make of that?" She

gave Edward an imploring look. "I can tell you're annoyed the police won't take me seriously about it being murder, and so am I, but please don't go making a fuss. I've decided the best thing to do is just sit tight and see what happens. Unless you have any better ideas?"

"To tell you the truth, Penny, I thought you would know better than to go sticking your nose into something like this. Let the police do their job. That's what we pay our taxes for. What makes you think you know better than them? It's no wonder the cranks are coming out of the woodwork to scare you. Nobody likes a busybody who's got too big for their boots, and ever since you were involved in helping to solve Julia Wargraves' murder you've been insufferable. If you're expecting sympathy from me, you can look elsewhere." He shook his head, exhaling loudly. "Quite frankly, I think you've only got yourself to blame."

Edward's words stung Penny more than if he had slapped her. She inwardly recoiled, regarding him in confusion. Since when had he become so cold and uncaring? Part of her wondered if that side of him had always been there, and she had chosen to ignore it. There were many people he didn't have a kind word for, for various reasons, but it was the first time she had been on the receiving end of such a diatribe, and she didn't like it. She pulled herself up on the sofa. "Please don't speak to me like that. There's no need to be so horrible about it. Whatever you think, you should be able to see I'm upset and I thought you of all people would give me some support. Your criticising me isn't helping, it's only making matters worse."

At least, Penny thought, Edward had the decency to look somewhat abashed at her comeback. "Look, I didn't mean to hurt you. I'm not good at pussyfooting around, and say what I think, you know that. Come here." He reached an arm around her shoulder and pulled her towards him. "Can we just forget I said anything?" Kissing her forehead, he added, "How about I promise not to tell you to pull yourself together and get a grip, and you find it in your heart to forgive me for putting my big foot in it?"

Penny leaned into his embrace. His turn of phrase could at times be unfortunate, she supposed, but that was Edward. He said what was on his mind, with no regard for anyone's feelings. At least he was true to himself. He had mastered the art of not caring what anyone else thought of him, something Penny often struggled with.

"I've been thinking, we should talk properly," she said, pulling back. She was careful to keep her tone even. "I thought we would have had the chance last night over dinner, but maybe we can have another try at clearing the air. I know things haven't been going well between us lately, and I'm hoping we can fix that. I didn't know how you felt about me helping the police before Christmas. If it bothered you so much, I wish you'd have said something sooner, rather than letting it fester."

"Would it have made any difference?"

"Probably not," Penny admitted.

Edward paused, his face softening. "You're right, we should talk it through. I was going to suggest I cook tonight, anyway. I realised after we spoke yesterday you always do the cooking, and that's probably why you were annoyed. Am I right?"

"Close."

"I even brought dinner with me," Edward announced triumphantly. "Ta da!" He jumped up and lifted the plastic bag he had arrived with, which had been parked on the floor at his feet. "I'd better put these in the fridge. No peeking."

Through the thin plastic, Penny could make out the distinctive shape of the microwave meals Edward favoured when left to his own devices in the kitchen, and she hurriedly called after him. "That's really kind of you, but don't worry. I had prepared something for later we can both have." She hadn't, but knew she had the makings of something more nutritious than whatever was in the containers in the bag.

Edward popped his head back through the archway. "If you insist. But let me do everything. I'll even fry my own steak, how about that?"

"I gave your steak to Fischer," Penny said. The look on Edward's face was worth the little white lie just for a second. Before he could answer, she began to laugh. "I was kidding, Edward," she soothed. "Just a joke."

Fischer, yapping and jumping around on the sofa, took that as a cue to play, and Penny held out a toy for him to chew on. He had so many scattered around the place, there was always one within reach.

Edward visibly relaxed. "Yes, of course. I knew that." Something outside caught his eye, and he peered out the window. "What's that idiot Monroe doing here? He's coming up the garden path."

"I'll get it," Penny said, Edward's displeasure evident. "Please, don't cause a scene. He's only doing his job, as you pointed out earlier."

"Hmmph." He followed her into the hallway, although he hung back when she answered the door.

"Hello, Inspector," Penny said just as her legs were knocked sideways by Fischer bounding past and leaping up at Monroe. She stepped back, grinning. "I think Fischer's glad to see you. Would you like to come in?"

The Inspector shook his head. "I won't, thanks. Just checking in as promised. Is everything all right?" Looking past her, he spotted Edward lurking in the hall. "Hello, Edward."

Edward replied with a grunt and disappeared back into the living room.

"Everything's fine, thanks." Penny caught her breath. Monroe was freshly shaven, and wearing jeans and a jumper, a woolly scarf and a casual jacket. His grey eyes were fully focussed on her, laced with soft concern. "As you can see, Edward's here," she continued, "so you don't need to worry."

A voice from behind her caused her to turn. Edward was pulling on his coat. "Sorry, Penny. I have to go back to the office. One of the partners just sent me a message, and he wants me to change something for the meeting tomorrow with HMRC. It's a high-profile tax investigation, and if it doesn't go well it could hurt my partnership prospects. You don't mind, do you?"

Penny shook her head. "Of course not. Will you be back later?" She remembered she had been going to ask him to check the van over but decided not to mention it. If she did, she had a feeling Monroe would step in, which would cause more tension with Edward. She was sure her father would be able to help instead.

"Not sure," Edward said, making his way out. "I'll call you when I know." He threw Monroe a glare on his way past him down the path.

Monroe paused for a moment, then said, "I should probably go as well. You have my number, promise you'll call if you need me?"

"Yes, thank you. Fischer and I will be fine," Penny said firmly. She eyed the golf club perched behind the door. There was no need to mention that. "Bye. And thanks again."

When both men had gone, she locked and chained the door. Lingering as she walked past the mirror, she tucked a strand of hair behind her ear. She liked what Susie had done with it and hoped she would be able to recreate the look herself, even if Edward had failed to notice.

"Well, it's just us again, Fischer. Now, how would you like some pretend steak?"

Nine

Katy Lowry, who was jogging past the cottage as Penny was leaving for work the following morning, gave her a quizzical look. "Morning, Penny. I didn't know you played golf." She continued to jog up and down on the spot while Penny closed the gate.

"This?" Penny said nonchalantly, as though carrying a golf club to work in a library was an everyday occurrence. She didn't mention she had also slept with it beside her bed. Penny had tossed and turned, staring at the clock for most of the night, the slightest sound causing her to stir. A creak on the stairs? She had convinced herself it was someone coming to get her. The rattle of rain on the window pane? Surely, a would-be intruder trying to climb in. There was nothing like middle-of-the-night anxiety to ruin a good night's sleep. PC Bolton calling before she went to bed had not helped matters, frightening her by bumping into the wheelie bin and causing a racket outside the cottage. "I don't, it belongs to a friend. Long story. Actually, have you got minute, Katy? I wanted to ask you something."

"Sure."

Penny's worries from the night before had evaporated with the morning light, and she was determined not to be intimidated by some coward hiding behind an anonymous note. "It's about Mrs Montague. She ate at the Pig and Fiddle the night she died. Were you working that night?"

Katy nodded. "I always work on Thursdays. It's busy at the quiz night, so the tips are good."

"Do you remember seeing her?"

"Yes. Only because she came in before the rush. She sat in the nook in the lounge, rather than the restaurant. I remember she said she would only have a small glass of wine with her meal, as she was driving later. When the quiz started, she was in the thick of it all, just how she liked it." Katy smiled at Fischer, who was dancing around her feet as if to mimic her jogging action. Looking back at Penny, she added, "She threw in a few answers to some of the questions even though she wasn't on a team."

"Did you notice if she was with anyone, or did anyone join her?"

"I don't think so," Katy said, short of breath. "She was by herself when she came up to the bar to pay her bill. But I couldn't be sure, Penny. Sorry."

"That's okay. Thanks, Katy. See you soon."

"I've got favour to ask of you as well, if you don't mind. I've finished the book I got last week, the one about the college student who has a passionate affair with the rich entrepreneur. I wondered if the other two books in the trilogy are available?"

Penny grinned. "We have several copies. I'll see what I can do before the van's back in Cherrytree Downs on Thursday."

"Brilliant, thanks, Penny." Katy ran off with a backward wave.

Penny unlocked the van and stowed the golf club across the front seat, Fischer hopping in beside it. Just because she wasn't running scared, didn't mean she was going to take any chances.

The routine of her working day was comforting. Rowan Downs, the library van's stop on Monday mornings, was quiet apart from half-a-dozen or so regulars. Penny took the opportunity to catch up on paperwork, including updating the list of overdue books. The mobile-library service was not computerised like the main library in Winstoke, making it necessary for Penny to keep manual records. It wasn't ideal, but Hantchester Council, whose jurisdiction the library service was under, had refused several requests for a tablet device that could be synchronised with the main library computer to make the process quicker. If Penny had a tablet of her own she would have used it, but it was something she had never got around to buying, and her ancient laptop computer wasn't up to the job.

A familiar voice greeted her as she was finishing up, and her face lit up when she turned around. "Hello, Mr Kelly. Have you come to take me up on my offer of first dibs on the new mystery books?"

Penny regarded Mr Kelly. The years had taken their toll on his weathered face, but his soft blue eyes shone in earnest. "Indeed, I have. I also heard about Myrtle Montague's generous donation to the library. I wanted to volunteer my services, if you need any help with cataloguing the books. I don't have a CV, just a healthy respect for the written word."

"I think I can take your retired headmaster credentials in good faith." She checked her watch. "It's almost lunchtime. Would you like to share my sandwiches, and we can talk? We can sit in the front of the van. Or, I have a blanket we can put on top of the bench, if you prefer to sit outside?"

The van was parked at Pike's Cross in the centre of Rowan Downs. The overnight rain had dried up, but she didn't want either of them to catch a chill.

Mr Kelly considered the options. "Let's get some fresh air." He climbed out of the van and shuffled the few steps to the bench.

Penny turned the key on the metal box where the fines were kept and closed the doors of the van. She removed a blanket, her plastic lunch-box and two small bottles of water out of the front, before joining Mr Kelly at the bench. Fischer scurried along at her heels.

"Here we go," she said, arranging the blanket on top

of the knotted planks and handing her companion a bottle of water. "I always keep a few of these in the van." When they were both seated, she opened her lunch-box and unfolded the greaseproof paper.

Mr Kelly peered across.

"I hope you like egg and cress." She offered him the box, pushing it towards him.

"Only if you're sure," he said, but he had already started to reach for a sandwich. "That's very kind of you."

"I'm glad of the company. Fischer isn't very talkative, so we have a lot of one-way conversations." She glanced down at Fischer, who was waiting to see if any crumbs were heading in his direction. "Good boy." She petted him. "Go play, and I'll fill your water bowl."

Fischer didn't need to be told twice, trotting off on the grass behind them, tail wagging ten to the dozen and nose to the ground as he sought new smells to follow.

"I remember Myrtle Montague from when I was growing up," Mr Kelly said, between bites. "She was a fine lady even then, always a kind word for everyone. And quite the beauty as well, may I add." He smiled, his face creasing in a myriad of tiny lines.

Penny sensed an opportunity to gently tease him. "Do I detect some romance between the two of you in the past?"

"I may have had a fleeting crush, but it was all on my side I'm afraid, and a long, long time ago, before I met my wife. In my defence, Myrtle was a few years older than me, so there was never any chance she would have looked my way," he said, wiping a crumb off the side of his mouth. "She was my sister's age, and I was the annoying little brother no one paid attention to."

"Was she from around these parts?"

"She was a cousin of the Pikes' and used to visit for the summer holidays and stay with her grandparents in the big farmhouse. Her family lived in Cornwall, and she had a wild streak we local children found fascinating. She could climb trees higher than any of the boys, and she skipped and played hopscotch better than any of the girls. We didn't quite know what to make of her."

"It sounds like she was a lot of fun."

"She was." Mr Kelly took a sip of his water. "Anyway, to go back to your original question, apart from the fact I was too young to be on her radar, she only ever had eyes for her husband-to-be. Once she started going out with Daniel, no one else had a look-in. Daniel Montague was quite a catch as well, I should add. He had everything going for him, money, charm, good looks as well as brains. I'd say there were a few young ladies with broken hearts when he took up with Myrtle."

"Surely no one would have held that against her?" Penny said. "From what I can tell, she was such a nice person it would be hard to be angry with her about anything. That's why…" Her voice trailed off. *That's why it was hard to believe anyone would have killed her.*

Mr Kelly's eyes narrowed. "Is there something you're not telling me, Penny?"

Just as Penny was deliberating whether to confide in Mr Kelly, they were interrupted by the sound of a black Land Rover pulling up at the side of the road. Inspector Monroe got out and approached the bench.

He greeted them with an awkward, but not unfriendly, nod. "Good afternoon, Penny. Mr Kelly." It was only when Fischer came bounding across the grass that his face cracked into a lopsided smile. "I'm sorry to interrupt your lunch, but would you have a moment to speak in private, please, Penny?"

"Of course." Penny got up and followed the Inspector to the side of the Land Rover.

His face was solemn. "Everything okay, Penny?"

"Yes, thanks." Penny had a feeling the purpose of his visit was more than just to check on her welfare, and it turned out she was right.

"I wanted to let you know Mrs Montague's autopsy has been completed and the coroner has decided no further investigation is required. There were indications of hypothermia, and concussion as a result of minor head trauma, the likely cause of which was hitting her head on one of the boulders in the pond. Given her age, the poor visibility by the duck pond and the slippery conditions, there's no reason to suspect foul play. It will be ruled as an accidental death."

"I see." Penny, aware the Inspector was studying her reaction, wasn't sure what else to say. A part of her was relieved, but another part of her was still reluctant to believe it.

When Monroe spoke again, his voice was gentle, but firm. "It's time to let it go, Penny. There was no murder, no mystery. There won't be any inquest. Whoever sent you that note is likely just a local person with a grudge about something. They wanted to rattle your nerves, and it worked. It happens sometimes in small communities where spiteful people have nothing better to do. Hopefully, nothing more will come of it."

"I understand. Thanks, Inspector. I appreciate you coming over to let me know."

"That's no problem. Take care, Penny."

She watched him get back into the car and drive off before she turned and walked back towards the bench. Mr Kelly threw a stick for Fischer to fetch, and by the time she sat down again, Penny had made a decision. "I'd love it if you could help me with Mrs Montague's books, Mr Kelly, but only if you accept some of the payment that comes with the task."

"Absolutely not. I'd be insulted," Mr Kelly replied with a frown. "If there's money involved, Myrtle intended for you to have it. I want for nothing and my outgoings are low. You can make a charitable donation on my behalf, if you insist."

He folded his arms. "But that's my final word on the matter."

"Fine. I'd be happy to do that." Fischer reappeared and dropped the stick on the ground at their feet. Penny picked it up and hurled it as far as she could, sending Fischer tearing off again. "The thing is, there's something else. Would you mind if I run it past you?"

Mr Kelly tilted his head. "Anything to do with Inspector Monroe's little visit, by any chance?"

Penny nodded, and began to fill him in.

When she was finished, Mr Kelly sighed. "I can see why you think there might be more to Myrtle's death. Although it seems as far as the Inspector's concerned, you should probably refrain from any more meddling, as he would likely call it." He paused, and his eyes twinkled. "Of course, he never said any such thing to me. Nothing to stop me asking around if anyone saw Myrtle on her walk the night she died, eh?"

Penny's face lit up. "Thank you, Mr Kelly. That would put my mind at rest. It's great to have you on board. Again!"

Fischer dropped the slobbery stick at her feet and woofed.

She leaned down to stroke him. "Of course, we're not forgetting you, Fish Face. You're the best detective of all."

Ten

Later that evening, sitting on the floor engrossed in a book about the history of The Detection Club, Penny came back to reality with a start when Celia peeked around the door of the library at the manor and said in a soft voice, "I'm going up to my rooms now, Penny. There's no problem if you're not finished, just close the front door on your way out. I'll lock up when I'm making my supper."

Penny, stretching out her arms with a yawn, caught sight of her watch and clambered to her feet. "I completely lost track of the time. Fischer and I should be off as well. By the time we've eaten and had our walk, it will be bedtime." She began to gather her things, stepping over the various piles of books splayed across the floor. "I should probably do more work and less reading if I'm ever to get this finished." The truth was she was in no hurry to finish the task at all. Lost in a literary world of discovery, she would be sorry when the books had all been sorted and sent to their various destinations. There was some consolation in the fact that books she had earmarked for the mobile library would be staying close to home.

Celia stepped into the room and took a treat out of her pocket for Fischer. She held it out near floor-level, and he appeared, as if from nowhere, to claim it. "Here you go, you little scamp," she said, releasing the treat with a chuckle. To Penny, she added, "Take as long as you like, I'm glad you're here. I can't get used to Mrs Montague not being around. Even though I might not have seen her most of the time, there was always comfort in the knowledge of someone else being in the house. Does that make sense?"

"Perfect sense. I like knowing Fischer's nearby somewhere, even when he's off doing his own thing." Noting Celia was much more collected than she had been at the weekend, Penny decided to broach the question that had been bothering her. "Celia, you said you didn't realise Mrs Montague wasn't home from her walk when you came back from the cinema, the night she had her accident. Did you not notice her Land Rover wasn't parked outside?"

"Of course. But as she was going to the Pig and Fiddle for dinner, I thought she must have had a drink and left the car in the village. She never would have driven after so much as a drop of alcohol. And she would have had no shortage of offers of a lift up the hill, I'm sure."

"That's true," Penny mused. The explanation raised another possibility in her mind. What if Mrs Montague's meeting had passed without incident, but then she had been murdered by someone who'd offered her a lift home? Someone who said their car was parked on the other side of the green, giving them cause to walk past the duck pond. "Can I ask you something else?"

"Please do, dear. I'll help in any way I can."

Penny's mind was whirring up a gear. "Once you're in your rooms, if Mrs Montague had come home and then gone out again, would you have been any the wiser?"

"Actually, probably not. It's a big house, and as I've told the women in my knitting group, as soon as I'm asleep a sledgehammer wouldn't wake me."

They were interrupted by a clatter from outside, and Penny was glad of the distraction. Having been warned off the topic of murder by Inspector Monroe, she didn't want to alert Celia to her thought process. It seemed to Penny, anyone familiar with the women's routine and living arrangements at the manor would know there was a good chance if something happened to Myrtle on her walk, no-one would be any the wiser until the next day.

Celia peered out of the window into the darkness beyond. "It's only James, carting stuff around in the golf buggy. He's been clearing some rubbish from the outhouses. Looks like he's knocked over a plant pot."

Fischer growled.

"It's all right little guy, he can't hurt you," Penny said, crouching down to settle him. "Fischer had a run-in with James the other day," she explained to Celia. "Why's he working in the dark? Would it not make more sense to do outdoor work during daylight? No wonder he's bumping into things."

Celia shrugged. "He keeps his own hours, just to be contrary as far as I can tell. I had a sharp word for him earlier, let me tell you."

Fischer woofed in approval.

"Why was that?" Penny asked, bemused at Fischer's vocal support for Celia.

"Mrs Montague had been on at him to clear the outhouses for a long time. It was a bone of contention between them. When I realised they still weren't done, I told him he should be ashamed of himself. He's been at it ever since. That woman was so good to him, and he never showed her a jot of appreciation."

"What do you mean?"

Celia's face reddened, such was her annoyance, and she let out an exasperated sigh. "He's supposed to do odd jobs around the place as well as the gardening, otherwise he would be out of work for most of the winter months. Mrs Montague never wanted to see anyone short of money, you see. He lives in one of the cottages on the estate, rent-free. Most decent folk would have been grateful for an employer like ours, but not James. He bad-mouthed her at every opportunity. Well, I've told him, I won't hear a word against her. She's gone now, may she rest in peace."

James, Penny decided, was well-placed to be aware of Mrs Montague's comings and goings, and was worth investigating further, especially if he and Myrtle didn't get along.

Celia walked over to the window and pulled the wooden

shutters closed, clicking the catch on the locking bar to secure them. A draught from the window caused them to rattle. "Master Milo will be home tomorrow, so that's something. Apparently, his wife's not joining him until later in the week, and I'm not sure if their children will be attending the funeral at all. To think of how long I spent preparing all those rooms, for nothing." She pursed her lips, the look on her face registering disapproval.

"What's Milo like?" Penny asked, snapping her laptop shut and stuffing it into its case. "I think I've only met him the once. It was at the Summer Fete, a long time ago." She tried to remember. It was when Ellen, Susie's daughter was a baby. Ellen had cried the whole day and Mrs Montague had taken the pram to give Susie a break, introducing Milo to her and Susie then. "Ten years, give or take."

"At least." Celia sniffed. "To think, he was such a nice little boy. I can remember him running around in short trousers as if it were yesterday. He adored his mother, and she worshipped him. She didn't want to send him away to school, but Mr Montague insisted. Said it would be the makings of him. Mrs Montague went along with it, but if it had been up to her she would have kept her son at home. Milo was always a mummy's boy and Mrs Montague was far too soft with him. In the end, he disappointed both of his parents. Such a shame."

Intrigued, Penny tried to keep her reply casual. "Really? Why was that?" She remembered her father's suspicions about a family disagreement, and Celia appeared to be referring to the same thing.

"I didn't see him much after he started university. He was accepted for a Medical Officer Cadetship in the Royal Navy. Did you know that?"

Penny shook her head. "I had no idea he was a doctor."

"He's not. He got kicked out of his medical course at university, and the Navy to boot. That was the start of it. The road to ruin."

Even Fischer had stopped in his tracks, ears cocked, as if waiting to hear what Celia would say next. Instead, she clamped her mouth shut as if suddenly realising she had spoken out of turn.

Penny made a mental note to try and find out what had happened to Milo in the years since. Celia had revealed plenty to be going on with for one night. And, with Mr Kelly having agreed to meet her at the manor to help with the books the following evening, she was confident their unofficial investigation was about to get off to a good start.

The man Celia introduced as Milo Montague to Penny and Mr Kelly the following evening, was so far removed from Penny's expectations that she hoped the shock was not obvious on her face. Slim and bearded, his physical appearance may have matched the handful of images she had found on-line from the limited research she had carried out so far, but that was where the similarity ended. Her father had always warned her of the folly of making judgments about people before meeting them and this was a prime example of how right he was.

The unassuming figure facing her in faded jeans and a scruffy shirt was at odds with the brash character she had imagined. Having uncovered Milo's penchant over the years for spending his trust fund drinking cocktails at the type of parties frequented by minor royals and covered by society magazines, she had expected him to exude confidence and charm, with a superior attitude to match.

In real life, Milo was softly-spoken and well-mannered. "Pleased to meet you both," he said, extending a friendly handshake. Surveying the books which they had begun to pack into the boxes provided by Celia, he continued, "I'd like to thank you for all of your fine work here. Both of my parents set a lot of store by the importance of reading, both for learning and enjoyment. My father said he sometimes preferred books to people, because they couldn't talk back." A wry smile stretched across his face. "I think that was one of the reasons we didn't always get along. I talked back rather a lot in my youth."

"It's a wonderful collection of books. It was very benevolent of your mother," Penny said.

"My mother was generous to a fault," Milo answered. "Material possessions meant little to her. She tried to teach me that money could bring great joy or untold heartache, but I never fully understood what she meant until it was too late." He paused, a veil of sadness shrouding his eyes. "If her legacy brings joy to others, that's all she would have wanted. I'm glad you can help fulfil her wishes." He picked up a dusty tome and opened it, reading aloud the inscription in the front. "'To Milo. The future holds such promise, that all the past pales in comparison. Daniel.'" He set it down again as though it were the most precious thing in the world. "Anyway, enough of my reminiscing. I hope to see you again."

The short meeting left Penny with a palpable sense of Milo's grief. He made his way out of the library with Celia as if he were carrying an invisible weight on his shoulders.

After checking the door was shut tight and the pair were out of earshot, Mr Kelly turned to Penny with a raised eyebrow. "He seems like a pleasant chap, considering what you told me about his past. Minor brushes with the law as a student are one thing, but he seems to have made unwise choices a habit ever since. It's clear he loved his mother though, whatever may have gone on."

Penny gave him a sorrowful nod. "True. He looked broken."

It was a guess which of Milo's actions had caused the family rift, or perhaps it was a culmination of all of them. Penny had discovered that after being dismissed from a prestigious university for possession of drugs (which Milo denied were his), the Montagues' only child had enjoyed a chequered employment history. The professional networking website Penny had visited indicated stints as a banker, manager of an art gallery and a wine importer. His current occupation was listed as historical researcher.

Milo's personal life was also somewhat of a roller-coaster. Having married a burlesque dancer in Las Vegas after a two-day romance, his parents did not attend the celebration when the happy couple returned to England. His wife was an occasional guest on a reality television show featuring rich housewives and had a love for the high life. It appeared the family lived in an exclusive part of north London, in a sprawling house that was most likely far too big for two adults whose brood of five children were away at school. Two of those children were not Milo's, but his stepchildren from his wife's former relationships. Last, but by no means least, his fondness for casinos and drunken partying over the years had led to a stint in a private hospital for 'exhaustion,' which Penny knew was usually code for something else.

Of one thing she was confident. Milo and his wife would be glad of any money he was due to inherit from his mother. The effort of funding their extravagant lifestyle would have exhausted anyone.

Eleven

Although she preferred to sit-in, Penny decided it would be wise to order her tea and cake from the Pot and Kettle cafe in Thistle Grange to take out. Fischer was off playing with his pals, the black lab puppies Daisy and Gatsby, and she had agreed to allow a group of ladies from the knitting group to take cover in the van from the rain in her absence. The wool shop, Spin a Yarn, was beside the Post Office where the van was parked and even though it was still her lunch-break, they had pleaded with her to take pity on them.

"The bus isn't for another twenty minutes, and we know you're too kind to leave us exposed to the elements," Mrs Wilkins had wheedled. "Please, Penny? Spin a Yarn and the Post Office are both closed for lunch. We promise not to touch a thing."

Having left Mrs Potter in charge, Penny hoped there would be no trouble while she was gone. The women's friendly bickering could turn nasty in the blink of an eye, and she didn't want any stock getting damaged in temper. Mildred Birch's hissy fit the previous summer had seen the library lose several books to a muddy puddle, and left Mrs Templeton with a bump on her head. When PC Bolton arrived to break up the ruckus, each had blamed the other for starting the argument even though neither of them could remember what it was about.

All was calm on her return, apart from a lost property issue. Penny had recovered all manner of personal effects in the van in her time, including a set of teeth, so she was used to it.

“I can’t find my glasses,” Mrs Wilkins moaned, running her hand the length of her nose. She scowled at her companion, Mrs Potter. “Look what you’ve done. It’s your fault, making me go into the Post Office with you to buy stamps. Why don’t you buy them at the newsagent’s, like everyone else? I’m going to have to go back when Mrs Dodds opens up again, and I’ll probably miss the bus.”

“Nonsense,” Mrs Potter said, squinting at her friend. “They’re hanging around your neck, dear, on that chain I bought you for Christmas.”

Mrs Wilkins raised her hand to her chest with a goofy smile and grabbed her bright red spectacles. “Oops, so they are.” She placed them on the end of her nose. “Show me that book again, the one by the British explorer who’s also a writer and a poet. Did you really meet him on a train?”

Penny smiled as the two women, old enough to know better, whispered and giggled about Mrs Potter’s brief encounter with the brave and rugged man of her dreams. The humdrum routine of Penny’s work at the mobile library had sustained her through the week to the point where she was no longer living in constant fear of a crazed stalker deciding to teach her a lesson.

She took comfort in the fact that Fischer had remained calm and was his usual playful self. She trusted him to sense any danger, and there was no indication anything out of the ordinary was bothering him. He still did tricks for treats and sulked if she scolded him, which was very rare, so there was no change there. Susie's son's golf club, although never far away, wasn't such a prominent fixture as it had been several days before.

"Hello, Mrs Nelson," she said to the stocky woman carrying a bag of knitting in one hand and a couple of paperback books in the other.

Mrs Nelson shoved the books towards her. "Here you are. I brought them with me as I'll be busy tomorrow, so I might not get to the van when it's in Cherrytree Downs. Wouldn't want them to be late so you can fine me again."

Ignoring the snide comment, Penny accepted the books. "Thank you. Don't forget, any time you need to renew books that's no problem. I'm here to help, not to make your life difficult."

"You could have fooled me," Mrs Nelson replied, not bothering to lower her voice. Penny noticed Mrs Potter and Mrs Wilkins had stopped their conversation and were listening keenly to the exchange. "Anyway, I'm going away to a warmer climate for a while, I can't stand this cold weather, so an extension won't be necessary. I have a lot to do before I leave."

Mrs Potter piped up. "Oh, when are you leaving?"

"Not until Sunday morning," Mrs Nelson said, peering outside. "Well, would you look who's here? None other than PC Bolton. Come to visit his little helper, no doubt." She gave Penny a withering look.

"Excuse me," Penny muttered, breathing in to squeeze past Mrs Nelson, who made no attempt to stand aside. After she had spoken to PC Bolton outside and assured him she was in no imminent danger that she knew of, she returned to the van, where Mrs Nelson was still staring daggers at her.

"Filed your snitch report for today, have you?"

Penny was taken aback. "I'm not sure what you mean, Mrs Nelson."

"I've heard you, asking everyone where they were the night Myrtle Montague died and if anyone saw her before she took her little swim. You think you're so smart, don't you, trying to find out if someone was out to get her?"

"Not really." Confrontations were not Penny's style, but the way Mrs Nelson was acting was making her feel very uncomfortable. "Where were you that evening, by the way, Mrs Nelson?"

"I was at the cinema, if you must know, at the schmaltzy Hollywood musical everyone's been raving about."

"I don't suppose you kept your ticket did you?" Penny said, feeling a little belligerent.

"Don't be ridiculous. I threw it away like any normal person would. One hardly keeps every scrap of paper on the off chance one might need an alibi! Besides, I was seen. Isn't that right, Mrs Potter?"

All eyes turned to Mrs Potter, who nodded. "Yes, Penny. I spoke to her in the foyer myself."

Penny felt a wave of regret at having fallen for Mrs Nelson's attempt at getting a rise out of her. It had almost worked. She knew people who had problems sometimes took their frustrations out on others, whatever the excuse might be. Taking a deep breath, she composed herself. "Mrs Nelson, for some reason I think we may have got off on the wrong foot, and I'd like to rectify that. I don't need to explain why PC Bolton was here, but I'd like to. Someone has threatened me, and he was making sure I'm safe."

A look of genuine surprise passed across Mrs Nelson's face, and behind her, Mrs Potter and Mrs Wilkins both gasped in shock.

"Well, I'm sorry to hear that," Mrs Nelson mumbled, a tad begrudgingly. "Now, if you don't mind, I'd best be off."

"When it comes to finding out what happened to Mrs Montague after she left the Pig and Fiddle, it looks like we've drawn a blank," Penny said with a sigh. She and Mr Kelly were in the library at the manor, finishing up after another evening's work. "We know she spoke to several people in the pub, but she wasn't accompanied by anyone in particular. She left alone. Then, apart from her speaking to an unidentified man wearing a green waxed coat at the end of the lane to the duck pond, there were no further sightings of her until her body was found the following morning."

"If we could identify the man in the waxed coat, that would be helpful," Mr Kelly said. "Also, I was thinking it would be useful to take a walk around the duck pond in the dark, to establish exactly what the visibility was like in relation to Mrs Montague's route and where her body was found. I'm wondering if anyone may have been lying in wait for her, out of sight in the bushes."

Fischer woofed, and spun around Mr Kelly's feet, wagging his tail.

Penny laughed at his reaction. "I think that's Fischer's way of saying you might be on to something, Mr Kelly. Either that or he misses his walks around the pond. I agree, following Mrs Montague's footsteps at a similar time of night is a great idea." A thought struck her. "The duck pond is still taped off, although I'm not sure why. There's no police presence now. I wonder if it's simply a case of them not having got around to removing the tape yet. I can ask PC Bolton about it tomorrow."

"He's probably the very person who would be responsible for removing it, so a reminder wouldn't go amiss." Mr Kelly straightened up and rolled his shoulders prior to tapping a cardboard box with his foot. “These are what we think are the valuable items, most likely to be of interest to the British Library,” he said, peeling a white sticky label off a roll and writing on it. He slapped it on the top of the box. “I’ve got a list of its contents and will contact them in the morning. There may be a few more works to add, but we may as well check if they want them as we go along. That way, if they don’t we can move those items into one of the other boxes.”

“That’s a good idea,” Penny said, thanking her lucky stars for Mr Kelly’s help. As well as being good company, she valued his opinion on what books would be popular with the mobile library customers. And, with his retired-head-teacher hat on, he was able to categorise the educational books better than she was into each of the key stages of the curriculum, and identify which college-level texts were out of date.

Without warning, they were interrupted by Fischer emitting an angry growl in the direction of the door. He ran towards it, growling again, his agitation increasing as he got closer.

Penny looked sideways at Mr Kelly. “I’ve no idea what that’s about. Did you notice anything??”

The old gentleman shook his head.

“Calm down, Fischer,” Penny said, walking over to the door and turning the handle. “There’s nothing there, see?”

She peered out and was startled when she spotted James carrying an antique chair down the hallway. “Actually, it’s James,” she said to Fischer, remembering her four-legged friend's dislike for him ever since their first encounter.

James turned around and challenged her, a sheen of sweat illuminating his brow. "Is there a problem?" His grainy voice was rough from years of smoking. By way of explanation, he added, "I'm taking the reproduction dining chairs to the auction house. Master Milo's orders."

"No problem," Penny said. "You startled Fischer, that's all. Sorry for interrupting you."

James grunted and lifted the chair again, and back inside the library, Penny closed the door with a click. "I don't think he likes us, Fischer. Don't take it personally."

She turned to Mr Kelly, who was pulling on his heavy wool overcoat. "Can I give you a lift home?"

"No need. My daughter is on her way. We're going to the pictures, to see…"

"…the Hollywood musical everyone's talking about, by any chance?" Penny completed his sentence with a grin.

"How did you know?"

"I think I'm the only one who hasn't seen it," Penny said. "Susie went last week. Edward and I sometimes go to the cinema on a Tuesday, but we didn't last night, as I was here. Not that he would have agreed to see that movie, come to think of it. He hates anything with singing or dancing in it." She hadn't heard from Edward since the weekend, which was unusual, but she guessed he was still in a bit of a huff after their argument. Edward's memory was longer than an elephant's, especially if anyone had ever slighted him. He still refused to give any custom to the Bakewell, after they had accidentally shortchanged him one busy Saturday afternoon. Although he pointed it out at the time and they rectified it along with an apology and a cream cake on the house, the damage was done. From that day forward, in Edward's opinion, the Evans' were a bunch of crooks.

"In that case, you must come with us," Mr Kelly said. "I insist."

Penny shook her head. "Thanks, but if you don't mind, I'd rather not. I'm pretty tired, and Fischer needs walking. It's our version of quiet time before turning in."

Mr Kelly hesitated, seemingly unsure whether or not to try and persuade her.

"Please, off you go," Penny insisted. "I'll be done here in a few minutes. Celia's visiting a friend, so I'll see myself out."

A car horn beeped outside. "Very well. That'll be Laura," Mr Kelly said. "See you tomorrow. Same time?"

"Yes, see you then," Penny said with a smile, reaching for her hat and scarf. "And I hope you enjoy the film."

"Come back here, Fischer Finch," Penny hissed, but her four-legged friend paid no heed. Tearing along the corridors of the manor, she struggled to keep up with him, and eventually gave up. "I know you're keen to get outside, but I'll be there in a minute," she muttered to herself. "Another few seconds isn't going to make much difference."

When she reached the wide-open space at the front of the house with a grand sweeping staircase as its centrepiece, Fischer was nowhere to be seen. An open door and a crack of light indicated he had probably gone exploring in one of the reception rooms. Approaching the door ready to tell him off, Penny froze when she heard voices coming from inside. She could not see the person speaking, but she recognised the voice as Milo's.

"I'm not surprised my mother wouldn't sell the place to you, Nick. You epitomise everything she despised about the nouveau riche. It wasn't your money she resented as much as how you spent it, I imagine."

Creeping closer to the doorway, she peered through the crack. She still could not see Milo, but a second male figure was visible, lounging on the Chesterfield sofa. There, floppy hair falling across his face and his right ankle resting casually across his left knee, was Nick Staines. His aftershave was so strong Penny could not only smell it from where she was standing, it caught in the back of her throat. She swallowed, desperately trying not to cough.

"If it wasn't for me putting a good word in," Milo continued, "you never would have got the land next door. I managed to persuade her it would be good for the village to get some new blood in, and that the construction work on your house would create local jobs. If I'd known you were going to bring in building contractors from London, I'd have kept my mouth shut."

"I appreciate your help with that, Milo, but if you can't help an old friend out, who can you help? That's why I'm willing to step in and bail you out. Just say the word. Sell the house and land to me and you'll have the cash within a matter of days. How does that sound?" Penny saw Nick take a healthy swig of amber liquid from a chunky crystal tumbler.

"It's hardly a fair price, Nick. You know the place is worth a lot more than what you're offering." The displeasure was plain to hear in Milo's tone.

"It's entirely up to you, old man, your call. Go ahead and put it on the open market and see how long it takes to sell. You could be bankrupt in the meantime. Old piles like this aren't moving anymore. Economic uncertainty being the way it is, rich foreign investors are few and far between."

Nick paused and turned his head towards the door, and Penny took a step back, holding her breath. At that moment she spotted Fischer on the staircase and wagged a finger at him. Signalling him to come to heel, she could have hugged him when he silently obeyed.

"I suppose I don't have much choice." Milo sounded weary. "I'll be seeing my mother's solicitor after the funeral. It's just my luck he's away for a few days, but he can draw up the paperwork as soon as he gets back. I'd love to keep the place in the family but needs must. I'm going to miss it."

"Are you sure you wouldn't consider living here yourself?" Nick chuckled. "Once the conversion's done, I'll sell you one of the apartments at a good price."

"Yeah, I'll bet you will. I'm afraid my wife would divorce me if I suggest it." Milo sighed. "I suppose I'll have to let Celia know about this sooner rather than later. She's lived here for a very long time. I'm afraid she will be terribly upset."

"Not your problem, Milo." Nick set his glass on the side table with a clunk. "Any more of that scotch? Your father had good taste in whiskey, single malt, none of that blended rubbish. It's a shame your mother and I didn't get along, but I don't think I ever stood a chance with her. She'd made her mind up to hate me before she'd even met me."

Penny was horrified by Nick Staines' attitude towards Mrs Montague, and pleased to hear Milo berate him, albeit gently.

"That's my mother you're talking about, Nick, and I'll remind you you're in her home. She was a sweet and kind soul, which you would have discovered for yourself, if you'd taken the trouble to get to know her. I doubt she wished you any harm. She had traditional values, and certain ways of doing things, that she stuck to."

And very nice ways they were too, Penny thought to herself, her ears burning.

"Just one more thing," Nick said, leaning forward. "Are you sure there are no other beneficiaries in her will? I'd hate for anything or anyone to get in the way of our gentleman's agreement."

"I shouldn't think so. I'm the only family my mother had. We may have had had our differences in recent years, but she always put family first. I expect there will be small bequests to her godchildren and her various good causes. Oh, and something for Celia, no doubt. A brooch or piece of jewellery, something of that order."

Penny had heard enough. As she was planning on telling Mr Kelly when she saw him, Milo seemed more friendly with Nick than being neighbours would warrant, and she wondered how that had come about. As she was leaving, she noticed a green waxed jacket hanging on the coat stand near the door. What were the chances, she asked herself, of Milo or Nick being the mysterious man Myrtle had been speaking to just before she died?

There were so many things running through her mind on her way home it was impossible to fathom that a short while later they would all be displaced, and it would be something else entirely that would keep her awake all night. Bombshells have a habit of doing that, she realised afterwards.

Susie's name flashed up on the screen of her phone not long after she had eaten. She was in two minds about answering, given the hour, but a sixth sense that it was important made her pick up.

"Susie, is everything all right?"

"No. I'm coming over."

Waiting for Susie to arrive, Penny put the kettle on, bracing herself for a late night. Whatever Susie's latest divorce woes might transpire to be, Penny would listen and reassure her friend for as long as it took to calm her down.

One look at Susie's face when she opened the door told Penny she had misread the situation entirely. Susie was there to support her.

"There's no nice way to say this," Susie began, when Penny was seated on the sofa, "so I'll just come straight out with it. Consider it like taking off a sticking plaster. A short, sharp, shock and then it's over with."

Penny gave her a pointed look. "Are you going tell me what you're talking about?"

"Oh, Penny. It's that toad, Edward. I've just seen him canoodling with another woman."

Twelve

Lying in bed the following morning, Penny replayed the conversation with Susie.

Canoodling?

She had almost laughed at the absurdity of the old fashioned term, and what had to be a mistake on her friend's part. "I don't think Edward knows what that means. Or, if he does, I'm not aware of him ever having put it into practice. It's exactly the sort of behaviour he abhors in other people."

Try as she might she could not recall Edward, he of the stiff upper lip, ever having engaged in a public display of affection during the whole time they had been together. The closest he had got to it was probably on their first date, when he had told her how pretty she looked, and at one point during the evening had tenderly tucked a stray strand of hair behind her ear.

Thinking about it made her chest tighten, and she threw back the duvet, resisting the urge to stay under the covers and never get up again.

She felt bad for Susie, who had anguish etched across her

face while she described seeing Edward dining in the French bistro, engrossed in conversation with a pretty blonde. Young, slim, immaculately made-up and expensively dressed, his mystery companion sounded like all the things Penny was not. Although she didn't aspire to be someone who was judged by their appearance over substance. However, she had thought better of Edward than to have his head swayed so easily. There were, it seemed, so many things she didn't know about him, or had subconsciously chosen to ignore.

Instinctively, Fischer had jumped into her lap during Susie's recounting of driving past the bistro and catching sight of Edward and the blonde sitting at a table in the window. "Are you sure it was him?" Penny rubbed her hand down Fischer's back with smooth, methodical strokes.

"Definitely." Susie frowned. "I was stopped at the traffic lights, and something made me glance in. When I spotted him, I thought you must be with him, so naturally I waved."

Penny groaned. "Don't tell me he saw you?"

"Not at that point. He was too busy gazing into her eyes and trailing his finger down the inside of her arm."

The only time Edward had got close to stroking Penny's arm was to awkwardly flick a fly off her perspiring skin on a summer's day. "Next, I suppose you're going to tell me a flickering candle illuminated her glowing skin and perfect features, and she was giggling coyly at Edward's scintillating repartee?"

"I wasn't going to mention that, but yes, that pretty much

sums it up. I parked around the corner and went back and stood outside the window. That's when he saw me, taking a picture on my phone as evidence. Do you want to see it?" She started rummaging in her bag for her phone.

"No, thanks." Penny buried her face in her hands. It was small consolation Susie hadn't stormed the restaurant and given Edward a piece of her mind. Apparently, the only reason she didn't was because she was on her way to collect Ellen from her violin lesson and didn't have time for a scene.

"Say something," Susie pleaded with her. "Aren't you going to rant and scream, at least a little? If you're not going to say anything bad about him, I'd be happy to do it for you."

"Please don't. It won't help. I'm not sure how I feel right now. I can't believe he would do something like that. It's so out of character." She wasn't sure what surprised her the most, Edward's deceit, his willingness to go to the French bistro, or the open display of tenderness.

Susie's words began to sink in as Penny tossed and turned all night, wondering what she had done to deserve being treated in such a shabby manner by her fiancé. If she was being honest with herself, her annoyance was not directed fully at Edward. A lot of it was self-inflicted. By the time the alarm went off and ended her fitful sleep, she was under no illusions that she hadn't brought the situation to bear on herself. The only reason Edward had treated her so badly was because she had allowed him to, not that that excused him entirely.

Fischer, instead of lying in wait in his basket for her to wake him with a cuddle as was their custom, was peering up from the bottom of the staircase when she came down in her dressing gown and slippers.

"Were you worried about me, Fish Face? You sweet little thing." She bundled him up in her arms and gave him a kiss. "I'll get over it. You're my favourite boy, you know that don't you?" She walked through to the kitchen and set him down at the back door. After she opened it, Fischer ran into the garden to do his business.

If she hadn't quite allowed herself to believe what Susie had told her the night before, the truth sunk in when her phone beeped on the kitchen counter where she had left it to charge overnight. The screen showed she had thirteen texts from Edward, which, at that moment, she had no desire to read. *Unlucky for some*, she thought to herself, switching the power off.

She went about her morning routine on autopilot, putting the kettle on and soaking a bowl of porridge oats with milk before going back upstairs to get ready. As an act of defiance, she took extra care with her appearance, applying makeup and tweaking her hair with hot irons the way Susie had shown her, to give herself a confidence boost for facing the world. She knew where feeling sorry for herself would get her. Precisely nowhere.

"Let's go, Fischer," she said, fitting his harness and lead. She guessed her confidence trick must have worked, as his earlier over-attentiveness had been replaced by his familiar exuberance and excitement at going on their morning walk.

Outside, the bracing morning air hit Penny with a blast. She strode into the wind, Fischer delighting in the brisk pace, his little legs trotting just fast enough to always remain one step ahead of her. The way the elements stirred her senses was in sharp contrast to the dull pain she felt inside. There was no anger. She was hurt more than anything, but the fact she could not muster up any strong emotions regarding the man she was supposed to be marrying someday carrying on with another woman behind her back, told her what she already knew. Edward had known it too. They weren't right for each other.

Maybe, at one point, they had both believed they were, but that time had long since passed. Part of her admired Edward for having the gumption to take steps to leave their relationship, although not the cowardly way he had gone about it. And Penny? Had she forced his hand, so she could walk away leaving him as the bad guy? It was too early to come to any conclusions and raking over the coals wasn't going to change anything. The sense of powerlessness she felt as she was buffeted about by the wind was accompanied by a wave of complete clarity that what she and Edward had wasn't worth fighting for. And with that realisation came an underlying sense of relief. It might take her a while to get over it, but she would survive.

Stomping past the newsagent's, she was lost in a world of her own when a man exited and addressed her with a cheery smile. "Morning, Penny."

Her hair blowing across her eyes, she gave him a sideways glance, at first not registering who it was, until Fischer started leaping around in glee. "Oh, morning, Inspector."

Monroe fell into step beside her, a flicker of concern crossing his face. "Is everything all right? You don't seem yourself. I hope you haven't had any more trouble?"

It took Penny a few seconds to realise he was talking about the note. She forced a smile. "Not that sort of trouble. What has you in Cherrytree Downs this early?"

He cocked his head towards the green and tucked his newspaper under his arm. "I'm here overseeing the removal of the police cordon. The green and the duck pond should be open to the public again in time for the children going to school this morning. You'll like that, won't you Fischer?"

Fischer's response was to lunge in front of Penny towards the Inspector, causing Penny to tug him back before she tripped.

"See you soon, Penny," the Inspector said, stopping to cross the road.

"Bye," she mumbled, putting her head down and continuing on her way, back to her thoughts of a life without Edward.

"Fischer's very lively this morning, does he ever stay still?" Mrs Potter motioned out the van doors to where Fischer was playing fetch on the green with anyone who would throw a stick for him.

"I think he's just happy for the green to be open again." Penny stamped Mrs Potter's books, inwardly grateful to her furry pal for providing the entertainment for that morning's library visitors in Cherrytree Downs. She wasn't feeling very talkative and Fischer's antics created the diversion she hoped would make it less likely for anyone to notice her spirits were low.

Even so, her mask slipped when Katy Lowry returned her books from the previous week and looked at her expectantly.

Penny gazed back at her in confusion.

"Were you able to get the other two books in the trilogy for me?" Katy asked. "I've been looking forward all week to reading them."

Penny suddenly remembered their conversation from several days before, and her heart sank. "Katy, I'm so sorry. I completely forgot. I'll be restocking the van at Winstoke this afternoon, so I'll pick them up for you then. I can bring them around to the pub later, if you like."

"Don't look so worried, Penny. It's no big deal. Honestly."

To her horror, Penny found her chin wobbling, and she bowed her head, attempting to quell the sob that was rising in the back of her throat. How could she have forgotten something so basic? This was her job. She felt as though she had let Katy down.

Katy reached out a hand, her touch gentle on Penny's shoulder. "Please don't be upset. Really, I can get them any time."

Penny looked up and gave her a grateful smile, unable to trust herself to speak.

"Go on," Katy whispered. "I'll hold the fort if you want to take a break for a few minutes."

Outside, the light drizzle didn't bother Penny, it just about summed up her mood. Fischer, spotting her, came bounding over with a stick and dropped it at her feet. She couldn't help but smile. Lifting the slobbery stick, she hurled it through the air and watched him race after it.

"There you are, Penny. I was trying to call you, but your phone was switched off."

She turned to see Mr Kelly, who was carrying an eco-friendly shopping bag stuffed with paperwork. "Sorry, I needed to clear my head for a while," she admitted.

Mr Kelly greeted Fischer and sent him scampering for the stick again. Turning to look out over the green rather than directly at Penny, he asked, "Anything you want to talk about?"

She shook her head.

"No problem, but if you do, you know where I am."

"Thanks." Penny was touched by the way people such

as Mr Kelly and Katy, were so sensitive to her feelings. That was one of the things about living in a small community, for the most part, everyone looked out for each other.

"I wanted to remind you I won't be able to come to the manor tonight," Mr Kelly continued. "It's my turn to host the Old Fogie's book club. But I can meet you there tomorrow, if you're going on your day off."

"That sounds good. And don't worry about tonight, I probably won't stay for long." She sniffed. "I think I might be coming down with something."

"You'd better get back inside then," he scolded her kindly. "You're not wearing a coat. Would you mind bringing this paperwork to the house with you later as well?" He held out the bag. "I called the British Library first thing and went through the books we've earmarked for them. There were several they have copies of already, and I've noted them on the list, so they will need to come out of the box. And there are a couple of others they're very excited about and are hoping we can send as soon as possible. The library will have a courier collect them."

Penny accepted the bag and peered inside. "Excellent. Leave that with me, and hopefully we can get them off tomorrow. Is there something else in here as well?" She could see a thick envelope, and the bag was heavy.

"Yes. There's some photos in the envelope I thought Milo might like. They're from my sister's old albums, taken at the dances she and her friends used to go to. There are quite a few old snaps with his parents in them. I checked with my sister and he's more than welcome to keep whichever ones he wants. There's no rush in getting them back, I just thought you may as well give them to him when you see him later."

"That's very kind of you, I'm sure he will be very grateful. Oh, and Mr Kelly?"

"Yes, Penny?"

She wanted to tell him about overhearing the conversation between Milo and Nick Staines but decided it would keep until the next day. "Thanks again."

Penny stared at her phone, and then back at Fischer. They were parked outside the manor, about to go in. "Do you think I should call Edward?"

Fischer turned his head and pawed at the van door.

"I'll take that as a 'no' then," she muttered and put the phone back in her bag. Her errant ex-fiancé had continued to text and leave her pleading voice messages throughout the day, such that she was bombarded by pinging sounds when she had switched her phone on after work. It was a weight off her mind to be able to turn it off again.

As soon as she opened the driver's door, Fischer leapt across her and jumped out, racing toward the portico.

The gravel crunched beneath her feet as she walked to the entrance and Celia let them in.

"Hello, Penny. Fischer, are you coming to the kitchen with me?"

Fischer looked up at Penny with his tongue hanging out.

She chuckled. "You're no fool, are you? You know Celia has goodies for you in the kitchen. Off you go then."

In the library, Penny was glad to lose herself in a parallel universe, one where Edward Marshall didn't exist. Working her way through Mrs Montague's collection of books was an adventure with surprises and treasures waiting on every shelf. There was still another wall of books to trawl through, dust, meticulously catalogue and then categorise depending on their future homes, but she estimated with Mr Kelly's help they should get through it in another week or so. She supposed then she could start planning the trip she would take with the money she had earned, and she vowed to make it a good one, worthy of Mrs Montague's gift to her. Because of course it was a gift, however Mrs Montague had chosen to dress it up.

She pulled the sheets of paper from the bag Mr Kelly had given her and read his notes and comments. His precise cursive script was easy to decipher, and using a ballpoint pen she carefully checked off the final list of books to be sent to the British Library, against the contents of the box. She then verified the number of books in the box against the number of books on the list, just to be sure. But no matter how many times she tried, she couldn't get them to tally.

Even though she had taken the duplicate titles the Library did not want out of the box, there were several other works she was unable to find. One of those was a book the curator had told Mr Kelly they were very excited about. That it was missing didn't make sense, as it must have been there when he made the list. Deciding she was tired and probably not thinking straight, she was glad when Celia and Fischer arrived, Celia carrying two mugs of steaming hot tea, and Fischer chewing one of his toys, left behind on an earlier visit.

"Thank you, Celia. I think I'll call it a night after this," Penny said, accepting the tea and slumping into one of the leather armchairs. "By the way, there are a couple of books I can't seem to find. You didn't happen to move anything in here, by any chance?"

"Not me, dear, although Master Milo was in here earlier, you should ask him. He's gone to pick up his wife from the station in Winstoke and then he's taking her out for dinner. I told him I've heard good things about the French bistro. Have you been?"

Penny shook her head, at a loss for words. As far as she was concerned, the less said about the French bistro, the better.

The way Celia's mouth was set in a straight line indicated to Penny the older woman was not happy about something either. "I can ask him tomorrow if you'd like? but I'd prefer if you did it yourself, Penny. Truth be told we had words earlier."

"That's fine, I'll mention it when I see him."

Without waiting to be asked, Celia continued, "Told me I'd need to pack my bags, insomuch as the place is being sold and my services are no longer required." She gazed at Penny in indignation. "It's not entirely unexpected, but I'm surprised at the way he just blurted it out. He might have been a bit more sensitive to my feelings, considering anyone can see I'm upset enough as it is. The funeral's in a couple of days and it's all getting on top of me."

"Maybe it just came out in the wrong way. Milo strikes me as being quite shy, and he probably felt awkward about having to break such bad news to you. I doubt he meant to be so abrupt or tactless."

Celia raised her eyebrows. "You always think the best of people. All I know is, I'm not his responsibility, and all this is his now." She made a sweeping gesture with her arm across the breadth of the room. "He said I should make other arrangements as soon as possible as the new owner wants to start work on the place right away."

"Did he say anything about who the new owner is?"

"Hmmph. Him next door, judging by the fact he was walking around this afternoon with a surveyor. Next thing you know, the bulldozers will be lined up. Mrs Montague must be turning in her grave. I'll be homeless and unemployed, and what does he care? I've done this job my whole working life and don't expect I'll get another. Not much call for live-in help apart from nannies and au pairs these days. Nobody wants an old woman like me getting under their feet."

Any thought of Penny's own troubles was forgotten in light of Celia's woes. "What will you do? Do you have somewhere to go?"

"I have savings, I won't be on the streets." Celia straightened in her chair and jutted out her chin. "I'm not looking for charity, don't get me wrong. It's Nick Staines and that smug attitude of his that riles me. He's a man who gets what he wants at whatever cost, mark my words."

From what Penny had overheard from the conversation between Nick and Milo, she thought Celia was probably right. "This may be a stupid question, but can you remember what kind of coat Nick was wearing when he was here earlier?"

Celia nodded. "A green waxed coat with a brown corduroy collar. I've noticed he wears that when he's in country squire mode. When he's back and forth to London, he wears a suit, or jeans with a leather jacket."

Penny's mind was made up. It was about time she had a word with Nick Staines, to see what he had to say for himself.

"This way, Fischer." Penny said, gently tugging on the lead in the dark.

It was a few hundred yards from the manor to the glass building beyond the trees that marked the edge of Mrs Montague's garden. There was no path, and although the Staines' residence had its own driveway, accessing it involved driving back down the lane from the manor, along the main road until the next entrance, and back up the hill again. The shortcut across the garden was the quicker option, although perhaps not the most sensible one Penny decided as she squelched through the muddy grass. At one point she had to give her leg a vigorous shake to loosen her shoe from where it had been sucked into the earth below. Fischer stopped and waited for her to extricate her foot and recover her stride. Arriving on Nick Staines' doorstep with mud clinging to her legs was not her most dignified look.

The huge glass box masquerading as a home was illuminated from several different rooms within, giving it a checkered appearance on their approach. The glass had an opacity rendering it impossible to see through, and Penny wondered what it was like inside. Glancing around the entrance, no doorbell was visible. Just as she was about to knock, a booming male voice coming from a concealed speaker made her jump. "Who is it?"

"It's Penny Finch, from the village," she said, addressing the door. "I'd like a word with Mr Staines, if he's home, please."

The speaker crackled for a moment and then there was a click before it went silent. Penny glanced down at Fischer, who was looking up at her in quiet confusion. The door opened abruptly, and Nick Staines stood facing them, cigarette in hand, wearing cycling shorts and a tight sports top that showcased his taut chest and abs.

"Hello," he said, looking her up and down, his gaze lingering on her filthy shoes. "What do you want?" His greeting, if not exactly friendly, was not hostile either, and he seemed to be regarding her with an amused curiosity.

Penny shuffled her feet, realising she hadn't prepared what she was going to say. Her first thought, *'Did you kill Mrs Montague?'* was definitely not a good opening gambit.

"It's about the manor house next door," she said eventually, fixing her eyes on his.

He took a drag of his cigarette before exhaling in her direction. "What about it?"

"I understand you're going to be the new owner?"

"I might be, not that it's any of your business."

Fischer nosed towards the door, trying to edge his way inside, but Nick put a leg out to stop him. Apparently, they weren't to be invited in.

"You do realise, you're making a woman homeless, someone who has lived there for more than forty years? Maybe if you weren't in such a hurry to knock the place down, or whatever your plans for it are, you might consider how your actions impact other's lives."

"I'm just expanding my property portfolio," Nick said with a shrug. "If anyone is being made homeless, it's nothing to do with me. That's Milo Montague's doing, not mine. And for your information, I'm not planning on knocking the place down. It's a listed building, so that would be illegal."

"I'm pleased to hear you have a respect for the building

laws, Mr Staines." Silently she wondered if it extended to all laws, but in particular, murder.

"Right. Well, now that's settled, I'll say goodnight." He made to shut the door, but Penny stuck her foot over the threshold to prevent him.

"Just one more question, if you don't mind. Where were you a week ago, last Thursday night, if you don't mind me asking?"

"I do mind, but if it will make you go away, I'll tell you." His eyes narrowed, and he frowned. "I know who you are. None other than the busybody spinster from the mobile library, aren't you?"

Penny chose to ignore his question, assuming it was rhetorical. His opinion of her was irrelevant. "Where did you say you were, Mr Staines?"

He let out a bored sigh, and taking a final puff of his cigarette, tossed the stub past Penny's head into the driveway beyond. "I was in London, at a television awards show, if you must know. Check the guest list and the media coverage if you don't believe me. I got ready beforehand and stayed overnight at the hotel in the West End where it was being held. Call my assistant in the morning, and she'll give you the details. In the meantime, I suggest you and your yappy little dog go away and annoy someone else."

Considering Nick was already irked, saying anything more wasn't going to change the situation. Undeterred, Penny continued, "You should be ashamed of yourself, Mr Staines.

Bullying an old woman like Mrs Montague while she was alive. Is that why you befriended her son, so he could persuade her to sell part of her land to you in the first place? You've had the whole scheme planned for a while, I shouldn't warrant. Ready to pounce on the rest of her estate, as soon as she passed on. You must be happy now."

"That's it, I've had enough of your cheek." Nick's face turned stony. "Milo and I went to the same school, although I was several years ahead of him. Ever heard of the old boys' network? I don't suppose you would understand how that works, unless you're from a certain background, which you evidently are not. This is the last time I'll ask you. Please get off my property, before I call the police."

Fischer yelped, and Nick rolled his eyes.

Penny, drawing herself up to her full height, nodded. "Thank you for your time, Mr Staines. I won't bother you again."

"Good," he said, slamming the door in her face.

"Oh Fischer, that didn't go very well." Penny wasn't sure whether she should laugh or cry. "What an unpleasant man. We can rule him out as a person of interest considering his alibi, but I hope I never have the misfortune of meeting him again. Time to go home and get cleaned up, I think."

Driving back into the village, she decided to treat herself to a warm bath and a glass of wine once they were back at the cottage. Perhaps at the same time.

Thirteen

"Out you go, Little Man."

Penny opened the kitchen door which led into the handkerchief-sized garden at the back of the cottage and watched Fischer scamper off. The garden, still a work in progress, was bare this time of year, save for an irregular patch of grass surrounded by low-lying evergreen shrubs. She looked forward to the appearance of the shock of daffodils around the gnarled trunk of the old apple tree in the corner beside the wall, marking the start of spring. Squirrels loved the tree, even if it had never borne fruit in the time she had lived there. And it was a perfect spot for the housewarming gift she had received from Susie and her children when she moved in, a lopsided bird feeder, made by Billy and Ellen. Later in spring, she was hoping for a show of the bluebells she had put in the previous May. Albert Finch had assured her planting them in full bloom would guarantee success, although she was apprehensive, not having inherited her father's green thumb. Mowing the lawn and dead-heading the climbing roses on the whitewashed wall at the back of the cottage, was the sum-total of her horticultural capabilities, although she was eager to learn.

Penny rubbed her temple and winced. "We'll go for our walk a bit later, little man," she muttered. "I have a sore head this morning." After her bath the night before she had telephoned Susie, one glass of wine turning into several. Susie had made light of Penny's encounter with Nick Staines, which made her feel a little better about marching up to his door and all but accusing him of murder.

"Good for you, standing up to him like that. And who cares if he resents being asked where he was the night Mrs Montague died? At least now you know. It does look as if there's no story, mind you. But don't keep looking for one on my account. I'm still milking my last scoop, which, let's face it, may be my one and only, but if it means no more murders in the Downs, I'm fine with that."

"That's a good way of looking at it. I should probably forget all about continuing to investigate, I haven't discovered anything worthwhile so far." Whether or not she could, was another matter.

On the subject of Edward, Susie had made her promise she would not contact him without letting him stew in his own juices for a little longer, even though Penny assured her it wasn't going to change the outcome.

"Thank goodness. I'm so glad you're done with that man." Susie stopped short of saying she had never liked him, even though Penny suspected that was the case.

"He was done with me first," Penny pointed out.

Apart from her pride being hurt, she considered she had escaped the relationship relatively unscathed. Her overriding emotion was a sense of relief, which spoke volumes as to the state the relationship had been in toward the end. She was intending to speak to him to get proper closure, but only when she was good and ready. In the meantime, she would ignore his calls and texts. Letting the answer phone pick up on her land-line and setting her mobile to silent had solved the issue, for the short term at least. She knew she wouldn't be able to fob him off for much longer though.

Back in the kitchen, she made a pot of her favourite rooibos and cinnamon tea, because it felt like a day for spoiling herself. On that theme, she scanned the shelves of the larder, smiling when she found the heavy glass jar she was looking for. No porridge and honey that morning, instead, golden baked granola. Loaded with a selection of dried berries, shredded coconut, and mixed nuts and seeds, its secret ingredient was an infusion of runny light treacle syrup that gave the cereal a crisp sweet coating when baked in the Aga. She spooned a generous helping into a colourful painted bowl she had bought from a market on holiday in Spain and hummed to herself while filling a jug with cold, creamy milk.

Fischer came wandering in as she placed two chunky slices of wholemeal bread into the toaster and waited for them to pop back up. His head cocked on one side, and a quizzical look in his chocolate brown eyes, he seemed to be questioning this change in her habits.

She looked down at him with a smile. "I know it's strange, but I'm changing things up today. Sometimes, routines are meant to be broken."

After placing the granola, milk, and a mug of tea onto a tray there was just enough room for a small glass of orange juice. The buttered toast went on a plate on top of the granola bowl, to save her a second trip.

"It's called breakfast in bed." She said, lifting the tray in triumph.

Fischer, confused, wandered over to stare meaningfully into his empty bowls by the door.

Penny chuckled and set the tray back on the table. "Oops. Sorry about that, Little Man. I should have seen to you first. Here you go, and as a special treat, I'll save you my toast crusts."

After seeing to Fischer, it was with an air of decadence that Penny went back upstairs to her bedroom with the tray. Meals in bed were something she associated with being sick, her memory being of one or other of her parents bringing her up tea and toast or soup when she was unwell as a child. They would sit with her as she ate and feel her forehead with their palm and tuck her in when she was done.

Penny couldn't remember the last time she had been ill.

Climbing back in to her still-warm bed, her headache had all but gone. She switched on the battered clock radio on her bedside table and moved the dial on the top until she found Winstoke FM. She had owned the radio since her university days, and in recent years part of her had been hoping it would die so she would have to replace it with a digital model with a wider range of stations, but it showed no signs of giving up the ghost. Until then, tuning into the required radio frequency was trial and error, but when the crackles turned to the sound of the local weather report, she knew she had found it.

With the pillows propped up behind her and the tray on her lap, she ate her breakfast with one hand while holding a book in the other, flipping the pages between bites. Although she owned an e-book reader courtesy of her day job, she preferred the experience of a physical book in her hands. She felt the time would probably arrive when physical books would become extinct, but she hoped it was a long time in the future.

At some point between hearing the traffic report on the radio and debating whether to go back downstairs to make more tea, she heard a yap from Fischer. Turning, she saw him standing in the bedroom doorway.

"Well, you took your time, have you come for your toast?"

Fischer barreled into the room and sat obediently on the rug at Penny's command, patiently waiting for the promised treats, and taking them gently from her hand as she held them out.

Penny was contemplating whether Fischer could be trusted upstairs by himself if she went back down to the kitchen, when there was a sharp rap on the front door. She momentarily froze.

"Ssh." Raising a finger to her mouth, she stared at Fischer, who she could see was itching to move. In a whisper, she added, "It's probably Edward. If you give the game away, I'll have to talk to him. Be quiet and let him think we're out on our walk. If he tries to find us in the village, he'll be out of luck."

The rapping on the door started up again, louder this time. Fischer jumped up onto all fours and started dancing around, yipping excitedly.

"Fischer! Come over here." Penny patted the bed. If Fischer made any more noise or went running down to the door, she was done for. Greeting Edward in her fleece pyjamas, with an extreme case of bed-head was not how she envisaged their showdown.

Edward, it seemed, had other ideas. It was all Penny could do to stop Fischer jumping out of her arms after he had joined her on the bed when the door knocker rattled once more.

"Honestly, that man is unbelievable." Penny let Fischer out of her grasp and got out of bed. One look in the mirror and her mind was made up. There was no way she was having any sort of conversation with anyone looking like this. And who, if not Edward, would think nothing of banging someone's door down at eight in the morning?

She walked across the room and hauled up the sash. Shouting out of windows wasn't something she normally did, but there was no getting through to someone like Edward. She had let him walk all over her for far too long. Now was the time to make it clear she had had enough.

Leaning out of the window, she shouted down. "Edward, please go away! Can't you just leave me alone? I thought I'd made it clear I don't want to speak to you right now."

Her mouth fell open as a man walked into view and a pair of steely eyes looked up at her.

She gulped. "Good morning, Inspector. I'll be down in a moment."

Penny glanced around the bedroom for Fischer, but he had already bolted. She inwardly berated herself for not having recognised his excitement at their early-morning guest. She should have known Edward never got a welcome like that from Fischer.

Considering she had already kept the Inspector waiting for several minutes, she hurriedly pulled on her dressing gown and slippers and went downstairs to let him in.

"Sorry about that. I thought you were someone else,"

she said sheepishly, leading him through to the living room.

"No problem. Happens all the time."

Penny motioned to an armchair and Monroe sat down, a bemused expression on his face. She wasn't sure if he was referring to the case of mistaken identity, or people shouting out of windows at him. "Would you like a cup of tea? I was just about to make some."

He hesitated, and then smiled. "Please. Milk, no sugar thanks."

Penny was glad of the excuse to escape to the kitchen for a few minutes to compose herself. Taming her unruly locks would be impossible, so the next best thing was to act as if she was completely unfazed at receiving company with her hair looking as though she'd just been struck by lightning. Monroe, meanwhile, who she could hear playing with Fischer on the other side of the archway, looked as dashing and handsome as ever, even at this hour.

She stirred the mugs of tea and took a deep breath, carrying them back into the living room.

"Thanks." Monroe said, pushing some books out of the way, so Penny could set the mugs down on the coffee table. "I'm sorry for calling on you like this without warning, but I've got some good news. We've solved the mystery of who wrote the threatening note. I wanted to let you know right away. It was James Donaldson, the gardener at the manor. We've been watching him for a while, but until we caught him red-handed, I couldn't say anything."

"Really?" Penny was confused. "Red-handed doing what?" She thought of the golf club leaning against the wall upstairs beside her bed and shuddered. She hoped he hadn't murdered someone else.

"He has been stealing valuable items from the manor. Mrs Montague reported several things missing before she died, and she suspected he might be involved. Since then, Winstoke Auction House and the local antique shops have been instructed to let us know if he brought anything in to be valued or sold. He got greedy in the last week or so since his employer died, and we've had several calls about him doing the rounds getting valuations. We caught him dropping a load of chairs off at the auction house last night."

It took a while for what the Inspector was telling her to sink in. "I see. I noticed some books were missing, but I thought Milo had taken them."

"That's what James was counting on. He realised he didn't have much time left to get his hands on as much stuff as possible. He didn't like you being around, before Milo came back. James knew his way past Celia easily enough but with you and Fischer at the house it made things more difficult for him."

Penny hugged her hands around the hot mug and let out a small groan. "He didn't kill Mrs Montague, I take it?"

Monroe shook his head. "He hoped that scaring you off would mean you'd give up the book categorisation work, keeping you away from the manor."

"I'm not scared that easily." Fischer came padding over to Penny's side, and she scratched his ears. "You had James pegged for a wrong'un straight away, didn't you, Fish Face?" She glanced across at Monroe. "Fischer didn't like him one bit."

Inspector Monroe grinned. "That doesn't surprise me, dogs are an excellent judge of character. I hope it puts your mind at rest about Mrs Montague's death. And as for anyone trying to harm you, there's nothing more to worry about. No need to carry a golf club around for protection anymore."

Penny felt the heat rising in her cheeks, something of a regular occurrence when she was around Monroe it seemed. She sensed a hint of mirth in his eyes, and realised he was teasing her.

Her face cracked into a smile. "I didn't think anyone had noticed. Good detective work, Inspector."

Penny had a spring in her step as she followed Fischer across the green later that morning on the way to her parents' house. Hands stuffed in the pockets of her padded anorak, she nodded in greeting to a couple walking a Great Dane. Fischer, happy to be back on his regular stomping ground, stopped at his favourite tree before he darted towards the path that led around the duck pond. Penny set off again several steps behind, pausing to let a cyclist past, and Fischer raced out of sight.

Despite the dark sky overhead threatening rain, she had come out without an umbrella, but nothing could quell the sense of joy she felt, not even a torrential downpour. Inspector Monroe's visit had reassured her. It was time to forget her belief the library card in the envelope had a hidden meaning, no one was coming after her and there was no point dragging things out with Edward either. She resolved to arrange to meet up with him as soon as possible. It occurred to her she wasn't sure who was breaking up with whom, not that it mattered, but after so many years together, it was only right they finished things face-to-face.

Suddenly Fischer appeared from the rushes, which grew at the edge of the pond, covered in mud, and bounded towards her, something glinting in his mouth.

Penny laughed. "What a dirty pup you are! I think a bath is in order when we get back. What's that you've got there?"

She bent down to retrieve the small oval object Fischer had dropped at her feet and turned it over in her palm. There was a pin on the back, and the front, although dirty, was unmistakable as a cameo. It looked familiar. Fischer gave a proud woof, wagging his tail.

Penny gasped. "You're a clever boy, aren't you? I think this is Mrs Montague's brooch. I'll give it to Milo when we're at the manor later. Even if it's not valuable, I'm sure he'll be glad to have it back as a memento. Well done, Little Man." She placed the brooch in her pocket and bent down to pick up a stick. "There's no point getting you cleaned up at Granny and Granddad's. You'll only go and do it all again on the way home, won't you?"

Fischer wagged his tail while she raised the stick and aimed for the rushes. No sooner than she had released it, he was off again.

Fourteen

"There you are, Penny. Come on in. I'll get a towel and clean Fischer; he looks as though he's been swimming in a swamp. Your father's in the kitchen. He was getting worried about you."

Penny stepped over the rolled up rug in the wide hallway, where her mother was vacuuming. Besides daily light housework, her mother divided the house into deep-cleaning zones, taking a different one every day. Friday was the hall, stairs and landing. By the time she was finished, the skirting boards would be gleaming, the banisters dusted and polished, and the carpets vacuumed to within an inch of their lives.

To Sheila Finch's dismay, Penny had not inherited her tidy gene. "I don't know how you ever find anything," she was wont to comment when she visited Penny's cottage. "All these piles of stuff everywhere make me want to lie down."

To Penny, the piles made perfect sense. She had her own little system and knew pretty much where to find anything. Attempting to explain that to her mother though was futile. When it came to organisation, it was Sheila's way or nothing.

"Hi, Dad."

Her father was sitting at the kitchen table, cleaning his pipe.

Penny pulled off her jacket. "Why are you doing that? I thought you gave up smoking years ago?" She walked over to the kitchen counter and lifting the kettle, filled it at the sink.

"All the more reason to clean it." Albert poked a pipe cleaner down the shaft. "It gets dusty in its box, you know. I might need it again someday."

"On one of your extended trips to the shed at the bottom of the garden, by any chance?"

Albert's shed was out of bounds to both Sheila and Penny, although Fischer was allowed in. Albert said he liked to get away for some peace and quiet, even though there was plenty of room in the house. It wasn't as though he and Sheila were under each other's feet all day. Penny had long suspected he went for a sneaky smoke down there, thinking his wife was none the wiser. It was more likely that Sheila simply turned a blind eye for a quiet life.

"I know what you're thinking," Albert said with an amiable wink. "Don't tell your mother."

"Tell your mother what?" Sheila called from the hallway.

"Nothing, dear. You carry on."

The blast of the vacuum cleaner started up again and Albert indicated to Penny to close the door. "You're late this morning. The school bell has already gone for morning break. Everything all right?"

"Yes. I just had a lie-in, that's all."

A look of surprise crossed her father's face. "That's not like you."

Penny shrugged and gave him a half-smile. She usually told her parents everything, but she wasn't sure if she was ready to discuss her relationship situation. If she relayed what Susie had seen, her father was certain to come down on Edward like a ton of bricks. It didn't seem fair, not having given Edward the chance to tell his side of the story.

She paused, and the kettle clicked off. "Tea?"

Albert harrumphed. "Fine. Tea's your answer to everything. Change the subject if you must, I expect you'll come clean when you're good and ready. How's the murder investigation coming along, by the way?"

"What murder?" Penny laughed. "I'm pleased to say the only murder seems to have been in my imagination."

When she had recounted her visit from Inspector Monroe that morning, Albert was pensive. "That's good news. As long as you're out of danger, that's the main thing. Nothing will bring Mrs Montague back, unfortunately. Get to the funeral early tomorrow if you want a seat. I expect there will be a big crowd."

Penny placed several chocolate digestive biscuits on a side plate and put them on the table in front of her father before pouring the tea. "Don't eat them all," she warned him, as he tucked into one with gusto.

"You'd better tell your mother to hurry up, in that case,"

Albert grumbled. "Not my fault if they're gone before she's finished doing the stairs." He lifted another when Penny's back was turned.

"I saw that," she said with a smile.

"George Kelly was telling me at our book club last night he found some old photographs of his sister's," Albert said when Sheila had joined them. "Said there was some of your mother and me in there." He smiled at Sheila. "Must have been when we were courting." To Penny, he added, "I'd love to see them, if you haven't given them to Milo already."

"I haven't even looked at them," Penny confessed. With all of the other things on her mind the previous day, she had totally forgotten about them. "They're still in the bag Mr Kelly gave me. It's up at the manor. I'll take a peek when I'm there this afternoon. I'm sure Milo won't mind if you want to borrow them for a couple of hours. If he's there, I'll ask him."

"If Milo agrees, why don't you bring them around later, when you're done?" Sheila added sugar and milk to her cup, the spoon clinking against the china as she stirred. "Come over for dinner. We've hardly seen you all week."

Penny hesitated. "I was hoping to see Edward tonight. We haven't arranged anything yet, but it's kind of important."

Albert raised an eyebrow. "Bring him along with you. He's always welcome here, you know, despite the fact he doesn't seem to like us. Luckily, your mother and I don't take it personally."

So much for keeping secrets. "I'm sure that's not true, Dad, it's just Edward's way. But it will be a bit difficult under the circumstances. The thing is…" Penny looked at each of her parents in turn. "We've kind of split up."

Albert spluttered on his tea.

"Kind of?" Sheila said gently.

"I mean, we have, but we just haven't talked about it yet. I was planning on asking him to meet me later." *If he's not got a prior date,* Penny thought to herself.

Sheila exchanged a worried look with Albert, who spoke up. "How do you feel about this, Penny? Are you okay?"

Penny lowered her gaze. The knot in her chest indicated the hurt was still there, no matter how brave a face she tried to put on. There was no disguising that from her parents. "I will be. But if it's all right with you, I'll skip dinner. I could drop off the photos later, though, and maybe you could watch Fischer for me? Edward's always been a little bit jealous of him, so it's best if he's not there." She glanced over at Fischer. "You don't mind, do you, Fish Face?"

Fischer was playing with a knitted draught excluder in the guise of a snake, and he ignored her, more interested in wrestling with his quarry than the conversation about his rival for Penny's affection.

Albert cleared his throat. "Of course, we'll mind Fischer. Do we have any sherry, Sheila?"

Sheila frowned. "Whatever for? Don't you think it's a bit early, dear?"

"It's never too early to toast our daughter's future." He reached across the table and squeezed Penny's hand. "Don't you worry. Everything will work out for the best. I won't ask the details of what happened, but I always thought you two were an odd match. You're too good for him, Penny. I'm just glad you've come to your senses at last."

"You sound just like Susie," Penny sighed. "If you thought so badly of him, why didn't you tell me? You've had six years to say something."

Albert gave the back of her hand another pat. "It's not for us to interfere, you're a grown woman. Besides I never said I thought badly of him, just that you didn't seem compatible. But I admit to thinking he is selfish and self absorbed, not the sort of man I'd wish you to settle down with. But we had to hope you would figure it out for yourself."

"I think I did, deep down, a long time ago," Penny admitted. "It just took me a while to face it. Edward's not a bad man, he's just a bit…" She struggled to find the right word. Arrogant? Over-bearing? Patronising? All of those adjectives were applicable, along with quite a few more.

"…of a plonker?" Albert interjected.

His wife admonished him with a stern look as he threw back his head and began to laugh. Penny and her mother exchanged glances, and then they too began to laugh with him. It was just what Penny needed.

Penny had intended to look at the photos as soon as she arrived at the manor, but was waylaid by Celia, who had other ideas, and pulled Penny into the kitchen as soon as she arrived.

"I suppose you've heard about James?" she said, clicking the door shut. She was baking, her apron covered in flour. "As if I don't have enough on my plate already. After the police were here earlier, *Her Ladyship's* only delegated more for me to do. Who does she think she is?"

"Oh dear. I presume you mean Milo's wife?"

"Indeed, I do." Celia lowered her voice. "I don't know where she gets all her airs and graces from. I heard she used to be a stripper, you know."

"Surely not." Penny didn't want to encourage that sort of talk, although to be fair, Celia was right. Burlesque dancers did take their clothes off, as far as she understood. "Some kind of a dancer, I think."

"Hmm, dancing around poles, more like. I've seen her on the television, pretending she's a fancy Nancy in that reality show, and anyone can see she's common as muck. Anyway, after that nice Inspector Monroe left this morning, *What's-Her-Face* called me in and said they'd like me to make a list of everything that's missing to help the police find the things James has already sold. If the stolen goods can't be found, then they'll need it for making an insurance claim."

"I suppose you're the only person who can do that, if James won't cooperate." Penny looked around the kitchen. Cake tins lined every available surface, as well as the large island in the centre of the room. "Are you feeding an army, Celia? It does seem unreasonable if they've asked you to do all of this as well."

"And pack my things and be out by next week," Celia reminded her. "Master Milo has an appointment with Mr Hawkins, the solicitor, when he gets back from his holiday on Tuesday." She motioned to the cake tins. "These are for the do in the village hall tomorrow after the funeral. The Pig and Fiddle are in charge of the soup and sandwiches, but I'm making the cakes. I want to do Mrs Montague proud."

"I'm sure you will, Celia." Penny looked down at Fischer, who was pawing her leg. "What is it, Fischer?"

He jumped up at her pocket, and she remembered the brooch. Taking it out, she handed it to Celia. "Fischer found this by the duck pond. I think it might belong to Mrs Montague. I wouldn't want anyone thinking it was part of James' haul."

Celia squinted at the brooch before passing it back to Penny. "This wasn't hers, I'm sure of it. It looks kind of familiar, but then I suppose it's a classic design. The only cameo Mrs Montague owned was a hair barrette she wore when she was much younger. When she started wearing her hair in a shorter style, she gave it to one of her goddaughters."

"I'll hand it in to the police station, in that case. Someone else might be looking for it." Penny put it back in her pocket, confused. She had been certain she'd seen this exact brooch not long ago, but then she'd also been convinced Mrs Montague was murdered, and that was way off the mark. As Celia said, it was a classic style of brooch.

Several minutes later Mr Kelly arrived and they moved to the library.

"Look at this one. There's your mother and father, with party hats on. I think that was at a Christmas dinner in the village hall."

Upstairs in the library, Mr Kelly handed Penny a black and white photograph. The festive decor didn't look much different to how it had been at the most recent Christmas party a few weeks before.

"They look so young. And my dad still had a full head of hair!"

"You're the image of your mother in this one." Mr Kelly handed her another. "Although the man she's talking to isn't your father, so best not show him that one."

Penny gazed at the picture of Sheila, who was engaged in animated conversation with a young man with long side-burns. In her twenties, she was dressed to the nines in a silk sweater, full skirt and pointy heels. It was hard to imagine her parents as she knew them now, being that young once.

"Is that Mrs Montague?" She pointed to a woman at the side of the frame.

"That's right." Mr Kelly's face lit up. "She really was a stunner, wasn't she?"

"Wow." All the young women looked pretty to Penny, but Mrs Montague was beautiful. Leafing through the photos, Penny was struck by how she was laughing in practically every one of the shots. She seemed oblivious to the stares she garnered from people around her, as though they were somehow drawn to her magnetism. "She and Mr Montague look like a couple of movie stars."

"Yes. Although, it seems like they've annoyed *her* for some reason." Mr Kelly indicated a woman who was glaring at the young Mrs Montague. "If looks could kill, eh?"

Penny gasped. She had seen that stare before, but it had been aimed squarely at her. Those same beady eyes, squinting into a purse full of money to count out pennies to meet a library fine. And the curled up mouth, sneering at her about how unfair the system was. The brooch on the woman's dress was the same as the one currently in the pocket of Penny's coat.

Mr Kelly gave her a concerned look. "Penny are you all right? Do you need a glass of water?"

Her voice came out as a whisper. "Do you know the name of the woman staring daggers at the Montagues?"

"Yes, that's Dawn Hampton. She was going out with Daniel Montague before he got together with Myrtle. The rest, as they say, is history. The Montagues lived happily ever after. As for Dawn, the story goes she was so brokenhearted she moved away not long afterwards. I heard she went overseas, although I'm not sure where."

"South Africa, by any chance?"

"Come to think of it, you might be right." Mr Kelly gave Penny a quizzical look. "Are you going to tell me where this is leading?"

Penny's heart was pounding. "Is Mrs Nelson's first name Dawn?"

"Yes, I believe it is." Mr Kelly held the photo up close to his face and scrutinised it for a long time. "My goodness, I see what you mean. The resemblance is uncanny. Dawn Hampton and Dawn Nelson could very well be the same person. Out of context and with so many years gone by, it never occurred to me. Are you thinking what I'm thinking?"

Penny nodded. "Probably. Let me show you something else." She got up from her chair and came back with her jacket, taking out the brooch. "Fischer found this today. I thought it was Mrs Montague's but Celia said not, but what if it actually belonged to the person who was with her on the night she died? The person who is wearing the same brooch in the photo you're holding, and who I saw wearing it on her coat at the library van?"

"I thought you said murder was off the agenda?"

Penny grimaced. "I know. But this…" Her voice trailed

off. Part of her wanted to let it go, but a niggling feeling was stopping her.

"I agree it's worth looking into. We really need to make sure one way or another."

"Yes, but it doesn't make sense. Mrs Nelson was at the cinema the night Mrs Montague died, Mrs Potter already vouched for her."

Mr Kelly clicked his tongue. "Convenient, but not conclusive. What else do we have?"

"Apparently, Mrs Nelson is going on holiday on Sunday. She was cagey about where and how long for. She just said somewhere warmer." Penny's heart began to beat faster. Perhaps they were on to something after all.

"I'll tell you what. How about we each see what we can find out about Mrs Nelson this afternoon? My daughter Laura has a friend who works in the travel agency in Winstoke, so I'll follow that up."

"Great." Penny lifted the photos and placed them back in the envelope. She wanted to study them again later in more detail. "Let's get going. I can give you a lift there now."

Then, after dropping Mr Kelly off and before any investigating, she knew she would have to do what she had been putting off all day. Etched in the forefront of her mind were two words.

Call Edward.

A sheepish looking Edward met Penny in the Pig and Fiddle that evening, still wearing his work suit. She had chosen the pub as neutral territory, and also as a potential source of information about Mrs Nelson.

There was no getting around the fact Mrs Nelson appeared to have a solid alibi. A word with Celia on their way out from the manor confirmed she had seen some of the ladies from the knitting group, Mrs Nelson included, buying sweets in the foyer before the movie. Penny had made no further inroads on the investigation that afternoon. On the walk past the duck pond on the way to drop Fischer with her parents, she observed the lighting, although dim, did not lend itself to people hiding unseen. If Mrs Montague wasn't alone when she died, Penny was certain she had been with a person she knew, rather than someone who had taken her by surprise. She had racked her brains to think of who Mrs Montague might have been going to meet that night and drawn a blank. There was still a missing piece to the puzzle, but for the moment, she had a different matter on her mind.

Edward stood up awkwardly to greet Penny, leaning forward with his hand stuck out, as though he couldn't make up his mind whether to kiss her cheek or shake her hand. Eventually he decided a peck on the cheek would be appropriate, but at the exact moment he moved in Penny turned her head and his nose butted into her temple with a crack.

"Ow. Sorry. Hello, Penny."

"Hi, Edward."

She sat opposite watching his eyes dart everywhere but at her. She couldn't ever recall having seen him look so nervous before, and it gave her no pleasure. The over-confident Edward was reduced to a quivering wreck, and all she could feel was sadness.

"I ordered you wine," he said, pushing a glass of white across the table towards her, spilling it a little as he did so.

"I'll just have an orange juice, if you don't mind." She said, thinking wine would be a bad choice under the circumstances. She started to get up. "I'll just go to the bar."

"No, I'll get it," he said, springing to his feet. "Won't be a minute."

Penny watched him at the bar, solemn-faced, trying to catch Katy's attention. The pub was busy with the Friday evening after-work crowd, but she knew it would quiet down in a couple of hours. The Pig and Fiddle wasn't the sort of place where people stayed for hours and got rowdy or drunk. Mellow and homely, most of the clientele lingered just long enough for a couple of drinks or a meal before heading on their way. She idly patted the wet patch on the table with a napkin.

Edward returned with her orange juice and sat down again.

"Thanks." She proceeded to sip her drink in silence, waiting for him to speak.

"I owe you an apology," he blurted out when he realised she wasn't going to start the conversation for him. "I'm sorry." He dropped his gaze, unable to sustain eye contact with her. "It wasn't supposed to happen like this."

Penny set down her glass. "You mean, I wasn't supposed to find out?"

"No, not that. None of it was meant to happen. One thing just led to another, and I didn't know how to tell you. I didn't want to hurt you."

"It's a little late for that, Edward." Penny's voice was calm and even. "But I think I deserve an explanation, don't you?"

He nodded, his face glum. "We met in December at a talk about tax fraud. I needed to get my professional education hours up. Renee was one of the speakers. Our paths crossed again the night of our office Christmas party. The firm she's a partner with was having their party at the same hotel. What a coincidence, eh?" He smiled nervously.

"Indeed." So, the sexy blonde had a name. And she worked in the same field, as a partner to boot. Right up Edward's street. "Go on."

"I introduced myself and told her how much I'd enjoyed her talk. I had a few questions, so we swapped numbers. It just kind of went from there." He shrugged.

Penny's cheeks smarted as if she had been slapped. The dreamy look in Edward's eyes when he talked about Renee told her he was smitten.

"I didn't want to say anything until I'd decided what to do."

"The thing is, while you've been playing both sides of the fence I've made the decision for you." Penny wasn't interested in whether she'd made the cut after his careful cost-benefit analysis of whether to continue their relationship, or to go all-in with his bit on the side. "Apart from the fact you've cheated on me and been dishonest to boot, I think we both know our relationship's not been great for a while." Had it ever been really great? He certainly had never had the same dreamy look on his face for her, as he had for Renee. But there was no point raking over old coals. They were where they were. "That's why I wanted to talk to you about it last weekend. Now, I can understand that you had other things on your mind."

Edward spluttered. "You're the one who was so wrapped up in Mrs Montague's book project and solving her non-existent murder, to pay any attention to me or what I've been doing. Clearly, your priorities lie elsewhere. Tell me, Penny, am I supposed to twiddle my thumbs, waiting for you to fit me in to your busy schedule while you're off playing Miss Marple?"

Penny took a deep breath. She wasn't going to tolerate being blamed for Edward's behaviour. She knew he really did believe she had been unreasonable, but that was still no excuse for what he had done.

"That's not how it should be, Edward. It's not my role to be at your beck and call. I'm sorry our relationship has run its course. It's just a shame that things had to end this way. I thought more of you. Unfortunately, you didn't extend me the same regard."

"Oh." Apparently, Edward was lost for words. If so, that was a first.

Penny pulled the diamond solitaire ring off her engagement finger and handed it to him. Immediately, she felt lighter without it.

Edward rolled the ring in his fingers. "If that's how you feel, I suppose we should call it a day. I was going to reconsider, if you'd asked, but there you go." He frowned, perhaps surprised she wasn't going to cry and beg him to come back to her.

She took a sip of her orange juice. "Yes, there you go."

He regarded her in earnest. "I hope we can still be friends. If you need any accountancy work doing, you know where I am. I'm sure I can arrange a small discount off my normal rate."

Penny nodded. "That's kind of you, and yes, perhaps we can learn to be friends again in the future, but at the moment I need my space. I hope you understand."

"Sure." Edward stuffed the ring in his pocket and checked his watch. "Are you going to be all right? I need to be off. I've arranged to meet someone. Do you want me to call Susie to take you home?"

Penny shook her head. Edward's concern was genuine, but she didn't need a shoulder to cry on. "You go on, I'll be fine."

"Well, if you're sure." He stood up and straightened his suit jacket. "Bye, then. Take care."

For a moment, she thought he was going to shake her hand, but this time he did manage plant a kiss on her cheek. "Goodbye, Edward."

Fifteen

Penny stretched out on the sofa, a throw covering her pyjama-clad legs. She dipped her spoon into the tub of vegan ice cream, promising herself to put it back into the freezer after one more mouthful. Fischer, curled up beside her, was chewing loudly.

"I'm glad to hear you're enjoying your Friday night dog treat. We're so rock and roll, aren't we, Fischer? I could get used to this."

She set the ice cream tub down on the coffee table and reached for the Winstoke Gazette. Susie dropped a complimentary copy through her letterbox every issue. With no Edward to dictate what to watch, a whole new realm of weekend television was opening up in front of her. That, and many more constructive activities, of course. But a feel-good television show or film would do for starters.

Distracted, she realised the ice cream was still calling to her. There was no point getting up from her comfy position and walking all the way to the freezer, she reasoned. That would involve disturbing Fischer as well, and besides, there really wasn't enough left to make the effort worthwhile.

"I may as well finish it, what do you think?"

Fischer's tail thumped against her leg, a sure sign of his approval.

Reclaiming the ice cream tub and spoon, she began to flick through the paper to the television guide. The movie review Susie had written for the Hollywood musical blockbuster caught her eye, and she smiled as she read the first paragraph.

'Opening night for the hotly-tipped Oscar contender was a sell-out at Winstoke Cinema on Thursday. Your intrepid movie critic, Susie Hughes, made it through rush hour at the popcorn stand and into her seat just as the opening titles started to roll. Only one solitary seat remained empty as she squeezed her way to the end of the row, thanking her lucky stars she wasn't the only straggler. But the delights of Hollywood wait for no one and the prime view seat was never claimed. What a waste! Someone missed a corker…'

"Typical Susie, always running late for everything. There's an idea. I might go to the cinema tomorrow night, Fish Face. Edward won't be coming around anymore, you see."

Fischer gave her hand a slobbery lick.

"Eww. Unfortunately, dogs aren't allowed in the cinema, so I can't take you." The movie had been open for just over a week, so the crowds should have died down. Going by herself did not faze her in the slightest. She decided to play it by ear, and check with her parents first if they were free to watch Fischer. "Let's see what Granny and Granddad say when we see them tomorrow."

Her phone buzzed on the table, and when she saw the name on the screen she answered right away. "Hello, Mr Kelly. How did you get on at the travel agency? I hope you had more luck than I did. I've nothing to report at all, I'm afraid." After Edward had left the pub, she had said a quick hello to several people, but she hadn't seen anyone with a possible connection to Mrs Nelson. "I'm all out of ideas."

Mr Kelly sounded excited. "In that case, I think you'll be very interested in what I'm about to tell you."

Penny leaned forward in anticipation. "I'm intrigued, what did you find out?"

Mr Kelly let out a chuckle. "I'm afraid the staff at the travel agent's might think I have a crush on Mrs Nelson, or worse, that I'm some sort of stalker. I said I had been talking to her about her upcoming holiday and it sounded fabulous. Asked them for prices for the same round trip she was going on and if there was any availability. Laura's friend didn't bat an eye. She pulled up the details straight away."

"So where's Mrs Nelson headed?"

"Cape Town, but here's the thing. She has an open ticket."

Penny exhaled. "You mean, she might not be coming back? Maybe she's waiting for the heat to die down before returning, not that there's really been any."

"True, but she wouldn't have known that when she booked it, which, incidentally, was a while ago. The travel agent asked if I would be staying with Mrs Nelson or if I needed accommodation." He chuckled. "She jumped to that conclusion all by herself. That's how rumours start, I suppose."

"Just out of interest, what did you tell her?"

"I said she'd best give me some hotel prices, just in case I didn't get lucky. The word will be all over the Downs before long."

"If Archie Cryer finds out, you'll be in next week's Gazette."

"That might not be the only thing in next week's Gazette. It gets far better than that." Mr Kelly's tone had turned serious. "Or worse, depending on how you look at it."

"Go on."

Even Fischer had his ears cocked at this point.

"I did some searching on-line and found some interesting history about our friend, Mrs Nelson. She made the South African headlines a couple of years ago after her second husband was shot dead by an intruder at their home in Cape Town. Mr Nelson was a high-profile businessman, and they lived in a gated community in one of the exclusive suburbs of the city. She wasn't home at the time, and subsequently made a televised plea for help tracking down the murderer. There was a substantial reward on offer. No motive was ever established, and nothing was stolen, despite the fact her husband was wearing an expensive watch and there were valuable art works on display in the house."

"Did anyone come forward?"

"Yes, but not in the way she expected. Someone who saw her on television recognised her from the theatre the same night her husband was killed. She missed the first half of the show and only arrived after the interval. Thinking the seat next to him was vacant, the man had left his coat on it. She had a few sharp words for him apparently, and the gist of it was she came out of it looking badly. Certainly not the softly-spoken, bereaved widow she had portrayed to the public on television."

"If she only got there at the interval, did that not call her alibi into question?"

"Indeed, it did. She said she was only a couple of minutes late for the performance and the theatre doors had already closed. No one was allowed to enter the auditorium after curtain-up. She had a drink in the bar instead and got into conversation with the bartender, who remembered her. No charges were ever brought as there was no forensic evidence and the murder weapon was never found. It's a cold case, but it does leave a potential question mark hanging over her head."

Penny's mind was working overtime. "If she was guilty, how magnanimous of her to offer a reward, she knew there wasn't really an intruder, and the money would never be claimed. It's quite clever when you think about it." She continued to voice her thoughts aloud. "We know Mrs Nelson was at the cinema the night Mrs Montague died, but she could have made a point of speaking to various people in the foyer beforehand, so they would remember seeing her. For the purpose of her alibi, she'd also have bought a ticket. Then, instead of going into the movie, she could have slipped out. If she got away with something similar once, why not again? I've just read Susie's review of the film in the Gazette which said there was one empty seat at the performance. We have no proof it was Mrs Nelson's, but the CCTV will show if she left early. What do you think we should do?"

There was silence at the other end of the line.

"Mr Kelly, are you still there?"

"Yes, Penny. I think Inspector Monroe needs to be told as soon as possible."

"I agree." Penny was already getting up off the sofa. "Shall I pick you up on the way to Winstoke?

"Penny, if it weren't for you, there would be no investigation. And Fischer, of course, finding the brooch like that, was quite remarkable. I think the two of you should go. It's getting late, and I'm going to have a cup of cocoa and call it a night. You don't mind, do you? This old man has had quite enough excitement for one day."

"Of course, Mr Kelly. I'll let you know what the Inspector says."

"Thanks. Oh, and before you go, I almost forgot. There's something else I should mention, about Mrs Nelson's first husband. Are you sitting down?"

Penny plopped back down onto the couch. "I am now."

"The unfortunate chap also met with an untimely death, falling overboard from a cruise ship after too much to drink. At the inquest, his grieving widow said he had mental health problems, implying he took his own life, but an open verdict was recorded. He owned a mine and left her a wealthy woman."

"Good grief, Mr Kelly, this is all beginning to sound unbelievable."

"Isn't it. But sometimes the truth is even stranger than fiction."

"It sounds like Daniel Montague had a lucky escape. If he hadn't fallen for Myrtle, Dawn might have made it a hat trick."

"If she gets on that plane on Sunday, she still could."

Penny looked around for the van keys. "I have a feeling Inspector Monroe might take some convincing, but I'll do my best."

To Penny's surprise, persuading Inspector Monroe there was merit in her theory about Mrs Nelson wasn't as difficult as she had anticipated, although that didn't mean he was willing to do anything about it.

They were in his office in Winstoke precinct, a small windowless cube, as no interview rooms were free. Glancing around, Penny thought if her mother had been there to see the towering piles of paperwork stacked on every available surface, she would have deemed the books, letters and magazines in Penny's cottage as amateur at best. Monroe had moved a box off a chair so Penny could sit down, and Fischer was snuggled on her knee.

"Hmm." He drummed his fingers on the desk, deep in thought, and Penny waited anxiously for him to respond to the evidence she had presented. Along with the old photograph of Dawn at the dance, she had also brought the brooch as well as the newspaper containing the film review penned by Susie. He spent some time scrutinising the photo, placing the brooch alongside it, before he looked up with a frown.

"I don't know Mrs Nelson, but if you and Mr Kelly are telling me she's the person in this fifty-year-old photo, I'm willing to take your word for it. You've done a good job piecing all this together, and for what it's worth, I think you could be on to something, but I'm afraid my hands are tied. There's no concrete evidence to support the police taking any action. We can't just go around arresting little old ladies every time they give someone a dirty look. The cells would be overflowing."

Penny's face dropped. "Surely, you can at least question her about her alibi? We've established a motive and found a personal item that puts her at the scene. If we can prove she was lying about being at the cinema the whole time, then she must have something to hide."

"I agree there could be something, especially given this

lady's marital history. I'd have to contact the South African authorities to get more information, but if she was never charged with anything, the fact her former spouses met with unfortunate deaths is neither here nor there. The brooch…" He shrugged. "I agree it looks the same as the one in the photograph, but we can't prove it was hers without forensic evidence. I'd be willing to bet there are a lot of women in her age group who have similar cameo brooches. I know my mother does."

"Yes, mine does too." Penny sighed, glancing down at Fischer, who was gazing at her with sad eyes. She knew how he felt.

Inspector Monroe was on a roll. "Also, even if the brooch does turn out to be hers, she could have lost it any time. The cinema theory is just that, a theory, and it won't hold water without camera footage showing the times she arrived and left the cinema."

"How long do you think it would take to check with the cinema, and is that something you would be prepared to do?"

Monroe was silent for a while. When he spoke again, it was with a tired smile. "I suppose I could look into it. But there are strict protocols to follow. I can start the process with the cinema manager, and I can contact my counterpart in South Africa in the morning, but there's not much time before Mrs Nelson leaves on Sunday. Forensics on the brooch are out of the question without a legitimate reason for the request, it's a costly business and our budget is stretched as it is. Besides it would take too long to get the results, and with no other proof we have no reason to detain her."

Penny's shoulders slumped. She knew the Inspector was right. She also had a feeling, if Dawn Nelson got on that plane on Sunday, that would be the last they would ever see of her.

Monroe was jotting something down in a notebook. "What did Susie have to say?" he asked, without looking up. "Did she notice Mrs Nelson at the cinema at all?"

"I haven't spoken to her about it. She mentioned she had seen the movie, but I didn't realise it was on the same night until I read her review this evening. Sorry, I've had a lot going on this week." Penny couldn't believe she had been so remiss. She had an awful feeling she was going to cry. "I'll call her quickly now."

She spent longer than necessary leaning down to rummage in her bag for her phone and by the time she retrieved it she was more composed. Swiping through the list of recent calls, she pressed on Susie's name.

"Hi, Susie, it's me. I can't explain all the details now, but I'm with Inspector Monroe. I'm putting you on the speaker phone, okay?"

Penny pressed another button, and Susie's tinny voice came through the speaker. "Sure. What's going on?"

Monroe spoke up. "Mrs Hughes, can you remember seeing Mrs Nelson at the cinema on the opening night of the

Hollywood musical you reviewed, by any chance?"

"I did, as it happens."

Penny's heart sank. She exchanged a look with Monroe, whose face was unreadable.

"She can't have seen the movie though," Susie continued, "She was scurrying out the front doors as I was coming in. I'm sure it was her. I was late, and she was the only other person around."

Monroe's expression flickered, meanwhile Penny gave Fischer a hug and he let out a joyous bark in response.

"Thank you, Mrs Hughes. I think that's all we need for now." Penny looked at Monroe for confirmation, and he nodded back.

"See you tomorrow at the funeral, Susie?" Penny said.

"Yes, I'll be there. Bye, for now."

"Now what?" Penny asked, turning off her phone, hardly able to contain her grin. "Can you arrest Mrs Nelson?"

Monroe placed his arms behind his head. "No. I'm sorry, Penny, but it's still too tenuous."

"I have an idea." Penny lowered her voice, and looked around, even though the door was closed.

"Yes, I thought you might. Go on."

"What if Mrs Nelson confessed? Say, if she were to confide in me tomorrow, at the funeral? And you just happen to be nearby and overhear the whole thing?"

"Entrapment, you mean?" Monroe sucked in his breath. "That's illegal."

Fischer barked, and Penny quieted him by knuckling his ears. "That's a shame. I'll be sorry to see Mrs Montague put to rest, knowing her murderer's walking free." She held Monroe's gaze long enough for his steely eyes to soften.

"Alright, you've made your point," he said at last. "I suppose we'd better talk this through. No promises mind you."

As Albert Finch had predicted, the village church was packed with mourners paying their last respects to Mrs Montague. The sun shone for the first time in days, not that anyone was surprised, the whispered word being that Myrtle had friends in high places. Cherrytree Downs came to a standstill for one of their own, and that day was no exception, the local scout group forming a guard of honour outside the church, and the Hampsworthy choir raising the roof on the inside. Vibrant floral arrangements brought a blaze of colour to the altar, and during the eulogy the vicar reminded everyone of the indomitable spirit and unrelenting kindness of Myrtle Montague, drawing happy tears as well as sad ones from many.

Penny hung back by the only door, having declined the offer of a seat from Dr Jones in order to ensure she did not miss Dawn Nelson on her way out. She reached out a hand to Celia as she passed by, one of the first to leave the church after Milo and his wife, following the pallbearers on the way to the graveyard at the rear of the church. Her parents had been sitting near the front with Susie, and would be some of the last out, and Penny motioned that she would see them outside.

"Hello, Mrs Potter," Penny said, falling into step beside her. To Mrs Potter's companion, she turned and smiled. "Mrs Nelson, how are you? I wasn't sure if you would be here today."

Mrs Nelson's reply was snappy. "Why wouldn't I be?"

"It's just that you said you were busy with your holiday coming up. How long are you going away for?'

"You're such a snoop, Penny." The older woman's face was twisted into a sneer. "Go and stick your nose into someone else's business, and stop bothering me, or I'll report you to that policeman you like so much." With that, she stomped off, leaving Penny staring after her in amusement.

"Come on, Fish Face. We'll follow a little behind and speak to her again in a minute or two. Remember, we need to steer her towards the big oak tree."

She waved over at Susie, who had just come out of the church, and was charging towards her like a woman on a mission.

"Care to tell me why you were with Inspector Monroe last night, asking questions about…"

Penny shot her a warning look. "Ssh. Don't say another word. I'll tell you later."

"Oh. Right, okay. Your mum and dad are talking to Mr

and Mrs Evans. They said to go on ahead."

They walked along the stone path towards the grave, where a large group of mourners were already standing. Suddenly Fischer swerved off to the left, dashing toward a giant oak.

"Oh, no," Penny muttered.

Susie stopped and stared. "What's Fischer doing? He's dancing around that tree like a mad thing."

"Probably seen a squirrel, I'll just go and check. I'll catch you up." She set off over the grass towards the tree, glancing behind at Susie, who was still watching them with a quizzical smile. "Go on," Penny urged her. "We won't be long."

"Righty-oh," Susie said, continuing down the path.

Penny addressed the tree in a low voice. "Hello."

"Hello," whispered Monroe, from somewhere out of sight.

She smiled and patted her leg. "Heel, Fischer. That's a good boy. Come on." Spotting Mrs Nelson wiping her cheeks with a tissue, she made her way to stand beside her.

"Not you again." She hissed.

"Afraid so. Can we have a word in private, please?"

"Absolutely not. If you've got anything to say to me, you can say it in front of my friends." Mrs Potter and Mrs Wilkins looked around and nodded in unison.

"I see. Let me just run something past you first, if that's all right." Penny leaned over and whispered in Mrs Nelson's ear. "Good act with the crocodile tears. But I know you killed Myrtle."

Mrs Potter piped up. "Everything all right, Dawn? Your face is a strange colour."

Penny nodded. "That's what I thought. I was worried. Why don't you come with me, Mrs Nelson, and get some breathing space away from all these people? Here, hold on to my arm."

Mrs Nelson gave her a beady glare, and let Penny lead her up towards the tree. Fischer darted off again.

"Penny Finch, I've had just about enough of your nonsense. Singling me out for bad treatment at the library is one thing, but this takes the biscuit. It was a terrible accident, how Myrtle died, everyone says so. I expect we'll never know what really happened."

"But you know exactly what happened. You murdered Myrtle Montague because she stole the love of your life, isn't that right? She married the man you wanted for yourself. And you never forgave her."

Mrs Nelson clutched her chest, eyes opening in surprise. She hissed back at Penny. "No, I didn't forgive her, and why should I? Daniel and I were happy. I've never met anyone like him, before or since. We might not have been together long, but he would have proposed, given time. Then *she* showed up and turned his head. Bewitched him, so she did. He didn't stand a chance. It doesn't mean I killed her, though. I was at the picture house, as I have told you already."

"Ah, but you never saw the film, did you? You made a point of going to the cinema and talking to people beforehand so they'd remember you were there. You even bought sweets, but then you left, isn't that right?"

"I went to get something from the car, that's all." Mrs Nelson looked away. "It's not a crime."

"I see. Tell me about your brooch, in that case."

"What brooch?"

"The one you lost at the duck pond, the night you killed her."

Mrs Nelson's voice cracked. "I have no idea what you're talking about. My cameo is at home."

Penny pulled the brooch from her pocket. "I never said it was a cameo, Mrs Nelson. But of course we both know it is."

"Give me that!" Mrs Nelson reached out to grab the brooch, but Penny was too quick for her, moving it to her other hand.

"Let's not forget your holiday, Mrs Nelson, and why you've left the return leg open. It's because you've no intention of coming back, isn't that right? I suppose it gets easier to take a life after the first time. I know all about your husbands as well, you see."

"Oh, for goodness sake you nosy little witch! I'll tell you what happened, but you'll never prove it and I'll deny ever having said anything. You think you're so clever don't you, but there's no witnesses here. Myrtle deserved to die, she had it coming. Making her out to be a saint doesn't wash with me. I'm only sorry I couldn't do it sooner, but I had to wait until Daniel died."

"Why?"

"He would have recognised me when I came back, of course! Myrtle and I only ever met in passing when we were young, and barely spoke. I emigrated not long after she got together with Daniel, and I dare say she never gave me another thought. That's why, when I asked her to meet me, she had no reason to be suspicious. I waited in the village near the shops until I saw her that afternoon and told her I had some information about that Mr Staines fellow, and not to tell anyone in case he found out it was me who told her."

A shiver washed over Penny despite the winter sunshine and her warm coat. Of course, she knew the ending of the story already, but that didn't make hearing the details any easier. There was no sign of remorse from Mrs Nelson, just bitterness.

"She met me as arranged, half way around the pond, close to the waters edge so we were out of sight. I asked her then if she remembered who I was, and she was shocked when I told her. Even more so, when I explained how much I hated her, and what my intentions were. Of course, she begged me not to, and said we could be friends. The cheek of her!"

"I'm sure she meant it," Penny murmured. "She was a very nice lady."

"Rubbish! I had the stone already picked out and waiting. Not too big to lift, but heavy enough to pack a punch. She fell exactly where I wanted her, straight into the water;

it was then just a small matter of turning her face down and holding her head under to make sure. She was such a little thing, light as a feather. I knew the pub quiz wouldn't be over for a while and no one was likely to find her till then, not that it mattered an awful lot. Doesn't take long to drown, you see. My first husband was gone in about a minute."

There was a growl from behind the tree, and Fischer appeared, followed by Inspector Monroe swinging a pair of handcuffs.

"I'll take it from here, Penny. Thank you."

Sixteen

A week later Susie handed Penny the latest issue of the Winstoke Gazette with a proud grin. "Hot off the press. Susie Hughes lands the front-page scoop, yet again, thanks to you." She pulled out a chair at Penny's kitchen table and sat down. "It's the biggest scandal to hit the Downs in years. Dawn Nelson, serial killer, who would have thought? I hope they lock her up and throw away the key."

Penny scanned the front page, even though she knew the story inside out. Dawn was being held in custody awaiting trial, and the South African authorities also wanted to question her again. "Somehow, I don't think she'll be going anywhere for a long time."

"Did they ever find out who the man in the waxed jacket was by the way?" Susie asked.

"The one who met Myrtle the night she died, you mean? Yes, apparently he called in at the police station and gave a statement a couple of days after it happened. He wasn't a local, just someone staying with friends for a few days. You know what Myrtle was like, always a kind and friendly word for everyone. Any word yet on what's to become of the manor?"

Milo Montague, as well as the rest of the community, had been shocked to learn he had not inherited his mother's property as expected. After learning the probable reason from Celia, Penny understood why, although it was not common knowledge.

According to Celia, Milo received the entire proceeds of the land Mrs Montague sold to Nick Staines after her husband died, to pay off his substantial debts. Mrs Montague had no wish to throw good money after bad and had warned her son at the time to clean up his act, which had not happened. As a result, the house and gardens had been left in trust for the benefit of the six hamlets and villages comprising Hampsworthy Downs.

Celia, meanwhile, had been given a choice of the furniture and gifted a sum of money to buy herself a house, she was looking for something in Thistle Grange.

As for the reason Mrs Montague left her library card in the envelope for Penny, she had drawn a blank. It had likely been a fortuitous but absent-minded mistake.

"There's talk of it being turned into some sort of private home for the elderly," Susie replied, "but it's too early to say for sure. I've also heard a rumour that might interest you."

"Oh?"

"Word on the grapevine is that Nick Staines is looking to sell up. Apparently just the idea of a load of geriatrics living next door is too much. I expect he envisages a constant barrage of complaints at his loud music and sordid lifestyle."

"Quite right too," Penny said. "The man's a menace and a bully. Well that's some good news at least. Let's hope the next owners are more respectable."

"Changing the subject, can I ask you something else?"

"Of course."

"Now you've finished categorising the books up at the manor, would you consider doing a regular Book Review column for the paper? I've spoken to Archie about it, and he's happy to take it off my plate and pay you to do it instead. Nothing too highbrow, mind you."

"That sounds like fun, I'll definitely think about it."

Susie's eyes narrowed. "Great. Listen, you're not pining for Edward, are you? Because I'd hate to think you're putting on a brave face about it and moping around behind closed doors. I know it's not easy going through a break-up, even if things weren't perfect before."

"I promise, I'm not. Fischer's been looking after me, haven't you, Fish Face?" Fischer, never far away, jumped up onto her lap and she bowed her head to rub her nose against his. "If anything I'm feeling relieved it's all over. It hadn't been a good relationship for some time, but after so many years together we'd fallen into a rut, and routine had taken over, it's just we hadn't been able to see it. I'm looking forward to seeing what the future will bring, and have lots of ideas for things I want to do. There's no need to worry about me, Susie, I really am fine, and if I'm not you'll be the first to know."

"Well we can be free and single together. Now I must dash, and don't forget to give me the scoop on your next case."

"I doubt there'll be another one, Susie," Penny said laughing.

"Don't be too sure, you seem to be a magnet for mysteries. I wouldn't be surprised if your next case is just around the corner."

"Woof!" Fischer, it seemed, agreed with Susie.

Finch & Fischer will return in —
Battered to Death

If you would like to be kept up to date with new releases and receive **The Yellow Cottage Mystery** (The prequel short story to the Yellow Cottage Vintage Mysteries) for free, please sign up to my **Readers Group mailing list** on the website: **www.jnewwrites.com**

If you enjoyed *Death at the Duck Pond*, please consider leaving a review online at Amazon

Connect with J. New online:

BOOKBUB

https://www.bookbub.com/authors/j-new

FACEBOOK

https://www.facebook.com/jnewwrites

TWITTER

https://twitter.com/newwrites

GOODREADS

http://www.goodreads.com/author/show/7984711.J_New

WEBSITE

https://www.jnewwrites.com/

Made in United States
North Haven, CT
19 June 2023